FAMILIES BROKEN

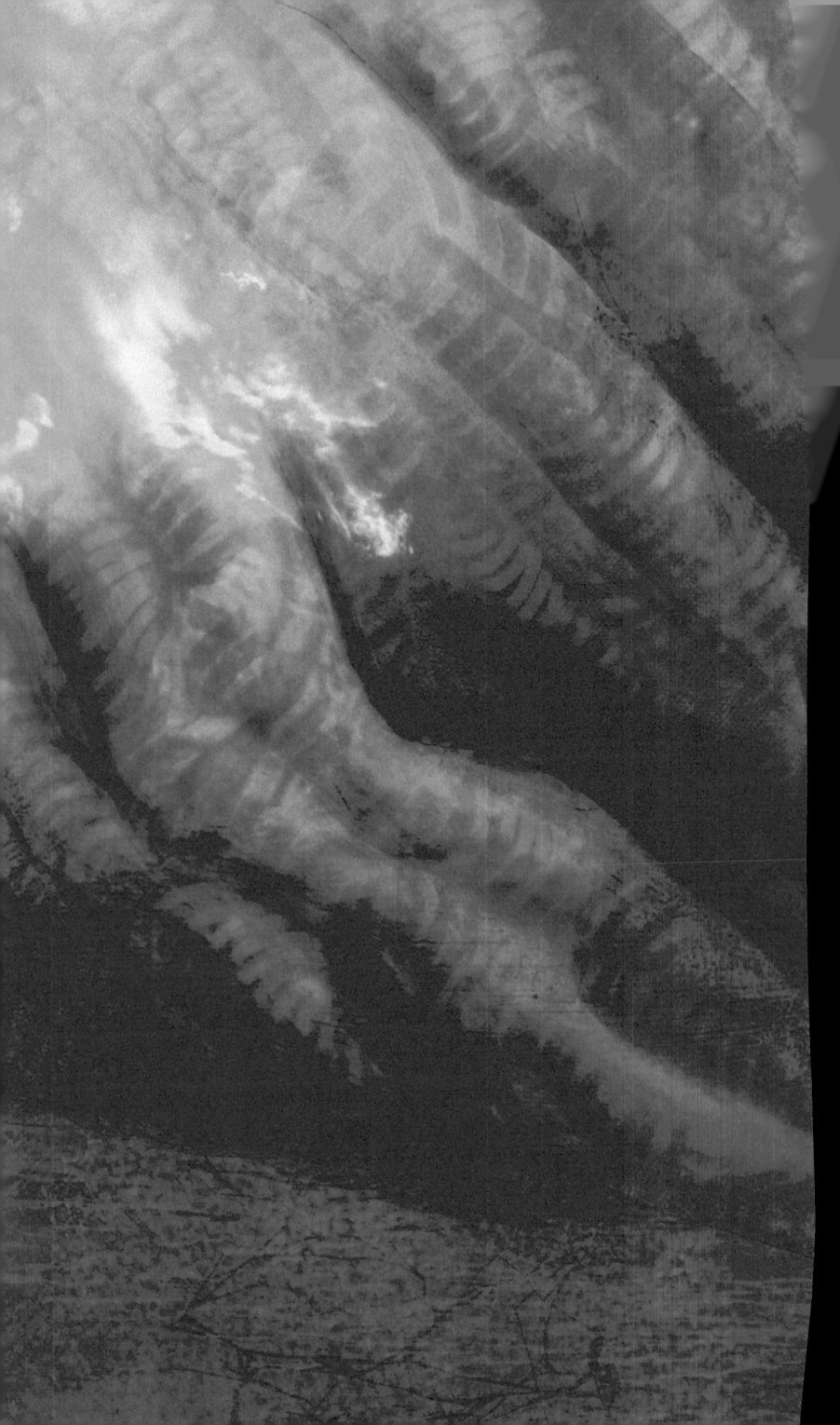

FAMILIES BROKEN

PC NOTTINGHAM

Families Broken
Copyright © 2025 PC Nottingham. All rights reserved.

Published By: The Little Horsemen an imprint of 4 Horsemen Publications, Inc.

The Little Horsemen Publications
℅ 4 Horsemen Publications, Inc.
PO Box 419
Sylva, NC 28779
4horsemenpublications.com
info@4horsemenpublications.com

Cover Illustration by Oxford
Cover Typography and Typesetting by Autumn Skye
Edited by Tabitha Saletri

All rights to the work within are reserved to the author and publisher. No part of this publication may be reproduced, stored in a retrieval system, or transmitted in any form or by any means, electronic, mechanical, photocopying, recording, scanning, or otherwise, except as permitted under Section 107 or 108 of the 1976 International Copyright Act, without prior written permission except in brief quotations embodied in critical articles and reviews. Please contact either the Publisher or Author to gain permission.

All characters, organizations, and events portrayed in this novel are either products of the author's imagination or are used fictitiously.

All brands, quotes, and cited work respectfully belongs to the original rights holders and bear no affiliation to the authors or publisher.

Library of Congress Control Number: 2025943864

Paperback ISBN-13: 979-8-8232-0972-4
Hardcover ISBN-13: 979-8-8232-0973-1
Audiobook ISBN-13: 979-8-8232-0975-5
Ebook ISBN-13: 979-8-8232-0974-8

DEDICATION

This series is dedicated to all of the children caught in the crossfire of adults who can't put aside their differences, especially to all the people whose families have been broken by war.

TABLE OF CONTENTS

Acknowledgments		ix
1	Sanu	1
2	Jab	6
3	Sanu	12
4	Jab	18
5	Sanu	24
6	Jab	29
7	Sanu	34
8	Jab	39
9	Sanu	46
10	Jab	52
11	Sanu	59
12	Jab	65
13	Sanu	71
14	Jab	77
15	Sanu	83
16	Jab	89
17	Sanu	95
18	Jab	101
19	Sanu	108
20	Jab	113
21	Sanu	120

22	Jab	126
23	Sanu	132
24	Jab	138
25	Sanu	146
26	Jab	152
27	Sanu	158
28	Jab	163
29	Sanu	169
30	Jab	176
31	Sanu	183
32	Jab	190
33	Sanu	195
34	Jab	200
35	Sanu	206
36	Jab	211
37	Sanu	217
38	Jab	221
39	Sanu	226
40	Jab	231
41	Sanu	237
42	Jab	241
43	Sanu	246
44	Jab	251
45	Sanu	257
46	Jab	262
47	Sanu	269
48	Jab	276

Book Club Questions.................283
Author Bio 285

ACKNOWLEDGMENTS

There are so many amazing people to thank for their support in bringing this series from a crazy idea into your hands: all of the wonderful people at 4HP who took a chance on me, Monique Bucheger, N.C. Scrimgeour, D. Everett Thomas, KC Woodruff, Kathrin Spinnler, Jaci Lunera, Martha Flick, Alex Bree, Elise Edmonds, Nico Vincenty, Hanna Day, Loren Huxley, Mick Vernant, Karim Ragab, N.E. White, AJ Braun, Tiffany O'Haro, and the whole Cru at the Radio Freewrite podcast (WebEater, Krispy, Murph, The Lotus, and Spud). They're all amazing creators and worth checking out!

1

SANU

Most ferocious among the invaders' troops were the knights belonging to the Barkheart Order. Nobody moved a sword or a ruler quite like them. General Ironseed confided to me that those knights invaded his nightmares as much as our land.

- Diaries of General Ironseed's secretary

Sanu gripped the lowest tree branch in his paw, halfway to meeting his twin brother. He didn't need the boost, but he accepted his brother Jab's offered bushy tail. In the days leading up to their parents' death a few months ago, they'd been at each other's throats, fighting and arguing more than ever.

After spending a month believing each other to be dead, and spending the last two weeks trying to reunite on this island, Sanu just wanted to accept the peace offering. A chill breeze passed through the hole in the ear that had been ruptured last week from a stray crossbow bolt, and Sanu was thankful for the balance Jab provided.

Jab smiled. "Some thinkers wrote that squirrels used to live in trees before we started talking and building things."

"That's ridiculous," Sanu replied. "Did those thinkers say anything more useful, like how to stop our home from getting destroyed by an unstoppable army?"

"No, but I have an idea." Jab waved his paws at the city's docks, where teams of rodents loaded supplies and armaments onto a fleet of ships. "*Alakazam!*" Jab placed his tail over Sanu's eyes. "See? They've all disappeared and now it's night time."

Sanu pushed his brother's tail out of his face. "Hilarious. But really, spending the last few weeks so close to King Ridgerd, I know how he thinks now. He's going to invade our home and force us to tell him about the local area. I don't want to tell someone about Qawar so they can invade it."

"I was trying to be funny, like you." The mirth left Jab's voice. "Thinking like you has saved my life a few times, believe it or not. Maybe we can convince Ridgerd to call it off. Do you think he's afraid of hyenas? We could tell him they roam the island at night."

Jab's darkening tone reminded Sanu of the horrors Jab suffered when they were first separated. He'd experienced a battle up close and watched rodents die, and then the scout who'd saved him was executed while Jab had to watch. Sanu needed to be nicer.

Sanu shook his head and gestured at the soldiers and sailors. "All of them believe conquering the Holy City will let them get the good afterlife, an eternity of happiness and peace."

Jab scoffed. "All you have to do for peace is to fight in a war. I'm not sure I'd want to follow that religion."

"Speaking of which," Sanu said, "look who's coming."

Sir Brouglas, the beaver knight who had saved Sanu and Jab's lives on different occasions, approached their oak tree. "There they are!" His accent was thick, but his skill in their language had grown. Even though the beaver belonged to a different religion and technically served their enemies, he'd been a mentor to Sanu and, more recently, to Jab.

Brouglas tapped his tail against the copper-tinted grass. "I'd join you, but you know what they say about beavers and trees. Come on down, lads, we need to get you on board. The king won't leave without you."

Using his tail to control his descent, Sanu slithered off the tree and Jab joined him.

"Sir Brouglas," Sanu said, "is it true you and my brother fought off a whole gang of bandits?"

The beaver waved a dismissive paw. "They were half-awake and we had the All-Planter's justice on our side, so it wasn't much of a contest. But I do have a gift for you, Jab."

Sanu glanced over at his brother who looked like he'd found a hyena in his bedroom.

"Um, th-thank you? I don't understand—"

Sir Brouglas reached into the fold of his overcoat and produced two books, both ragged from age and use. "I know it's not much, but when you said you wanted to take the oaths, I decided you should have these. I was so moved when you said you wanted to become a Sprouter after spending time with me." He lifted the first book, thinner than the other and filled with Frenglese letters that Sanu couldn't read. Even though he was getting good at Brouglas's language, reading it was hard because the letters were often stylized.

"This," Brouglas said, "is the journal of my preparation period before I took the oaths. I wasn't much older than you when I started writing these. This journal..." Brouglas sucked in a deep breath and steadied his voice, "helped me get through dark times."

"Oh, please," Jab said, waving his paws. "I couldn't possibly take that—"

"He's *honored*," Sanu teased. "That's so nice of you."

After Jab had claimed to defeat a bandit gang, his story about pretending to convert to their enemy's religion to escape a dungeon sounded fake. A smile curled up Sanu's muzzle, making his whiskers rise in tight arcs. "Jab is going to be the best Sprouter. Do you have a dictionary so he can translate your words into Qawari and read them?"

Jab shot Sanu the shocked glare they'd send each other when one of them tattled.

Brouglas's smile shone bright enough to shame the sun. "I'm glad you support him, lad."

He wiggled the second book, thicker and older-looking, "And Jab, you'll also need your own copy of the Ganandeeds. I know you know some of the stories already, but you should hear them from the Sprouter perspective." He sighed contentedly. "It makes me so happy to know you've accepted the All-Planter."

"Well, um, Sir Brouglas, Grovekeepers believe in the All-Planter too, so that part i-isn't new," Jab stuttered.

Sanu stepped between them. "Maybe Jab can read them later? I don't want to miss the boat, and I can't leave this island fast enough."

"Of course." Brouglas thrust the books into Jab's arms and then closed Jab's paws around them. "We've all had enough of Coppergrass Island. Yagub will give you a translation guide."

Sanu tried to send "I'm sorry" eyes to Jab, who wouldn't return eye contact. Sanu hated how much of a jerk he was being. He should've found a way to get Jab out of it instead of leaning into the joke. Sir Brouglas was really devout, and so was Jab. Being a Grovekeeper was the most important part of Jab's life. Sanu had only started praying a few months ago because he thought Jab had died and he wanted to honor him.

He'd find a way to get Jab out of this mess.

The three of them descended the hill toward Newhouse City's docks, and Brouglas pointed at the king's flagship. "I will warn you both that the king is in a foul mood. He's gotten news, and it is not good."

2

JAB

My journey in faith began in earnest at the Battle of Phranktonbourg. I'd gone to Gananhall each day as a boy with my brother, but it wasn't until I came to terms with how fragile life is that I turned to the All-Planter. I wonder if my brother ever came to the same conclusion.

- *From the prayer journal of Sir Brouglas*

The last time Jab sailed on a boat, he fell overboard during a storm. Setting hindpaw on the gangplank of King Ridgerd's sailing cog sent a shiver through his tail. The sea's salty aroma soothed his nostrils, and he debated staying behind. Coppergrass was a newly-liberated island paradise, but if he stayed, his home would be in greater danger than it already was.

He glanced at Sanu, walking on his right, which provided a full view of Sanu's mangled ear. The sight of his twin's ear made Jab's skin crawl. It looked like a crocodile or shark had ripped a piece of the ear off, but the reality was darker: a crossbow bolt meant for the king had ripped through Sanu's ear. Twelve was too young for a battle scar; he and Sanu had been playing with little kids just a few months ago.

When Jab closed his eyes, he still saw the flames and blood of battles, and heard the crunch of steel and bone as rodents howled. Jab could hide his emotional scars, but Sanu had to wear his forever. The war back home, and now their misadventure in Coppergrass, had taken so much from both of them. Jab wished they could go back to their old life with Mom and Dad.

But their old life hadn't been so idyllic either. Jab and Sanu argued constantly, just like Mom and Dad did, right up until the plague took them.

And back then, the wrong flags had flown over the Holy City.

Now that the right flags flew, Jab was stuck boarding the ship of a king who would replace the flags again.

"What's wrong?" Sanu asked, snapping Jab from his trance.

Jab marched off the gangplank, stepping onto the sailing cog. "Bad memories. I feel like I never left the battle at the lake."

"Hey, I'm sorry about before. I thought you were joking about becoming a Sprouter." Sanu offered a paw, and Jab took it. He didn't need it, but he liked letting Sanu think that he was helping. With a damaged ear messing with his balance, Sanu was probably the one who needed more help.

Jab glanced over his shoulder and saw that Brouglas was locked in conversation with his squire, a squirrel named Yagub whom Sanu had gotten close to in the last few months. "I had to tell some lies since I became a scout. I don't like it, but it's saved my life a few times now." Being dishonest about his own faith hurt more than the other falsehoods though.

Jab loved being a Grovekeeper. Reading the Divine Poetics wasn't enough for him. He memorized big sections of the poems and wanted to one day memorize the whole thing, and he read books by prayer wardens who explained passages in the holy books. So telling a lie about what was in his heart of hearts felt like the ultimate betrayal.

And he still hadn't told Brouglas the truth, which stung even more.

"You're doing it again," Sanu said.

"Huh?" Jab blinked hard and moved away from the gangplank, letting his hindpaws adjust to the ship's gentle bob. The sailors and soldiers preparing for departure did more to shake the wood than the waves.

"You're making that face where something is whirling inside and you pretend like it's not," Sanu said.

"Earlier, with Brouglas... I know you were trying to be funny. We had been joking around before. I'm not mad at you."

The ship's shaking grew more intense, and Jab's breath hitched. Thoughts of storms ran through his mind, but the sky was clearer than boiled water and the wind was barely a whisper.

It was not the elements or other sailors, but a hamster who shook the sailing cog. King Ridgerd approached. He hadn't wanted to stop at Coppergrass Isle, but while there, he had deposed the wicked baroness ruling it and fought off her army, leading his troops from the front. Sanu had told Jab about Ridgerd in a fight—his movements were graceful and horrifying in equal measures, and his strength and swordsrodentship were like something out of mythology.

And he was about to invade Jab and Sanu's home.

"There they are!" Ridgerd's voice was more friendly than Jab had expected of a king, speaking his language simply enough for Jab to understand. "I was worried I'd have to rip apart this metal-crusted island again to find you."

Some of the soldiers stopped to laugh.

The royal hamster smirked and pointed at the giggling sailors. "Though these lads know it would just be to get more of the island's food!"

Jab hadn't eaten much the last few days beyond the fruits Brouglas had scrounged for them. Knowing Sanu ate well with Ridgerd while on the island made a bit of jealousy flare in him, and his stomach growled.

Sanu chuckled. "You'd give any excuse to go back and see your new wife, I bet!" More of the soldiers laughed and raised their fists in the air.

Jab arched an eyebrow at his brother. They'd attended the royal wedding only a few hours before, and both the king and new ruler of the island were quite eager to depart from each other. *Why wouldn't a newlywed king want to spend some time with his new queen or to bring her with him?* A level-headed leader like her would've been a voice of reason and calm, which they needed more of.

"No," Ridgerd laughed. "I'm afraid my dear will have to await my return while she restores Coppergrass. And besides," Ridgerd turned to his troops, "I now share something in common with my brave pilgrims who have left their families behind for our most noble cause."

The laughs turned to cheers, and Jab remembered why they followed the king into battle. He also remembered that Brouglas had recently told them the king was "in a mood," but Jab hadn't expected this.

Ridgerd pointed to Brouglas and Yagub as they came to the top of the gangplank. "Both of you, come with me and the twins who can't seem to stay together. News came from Freng, and we have much to discuss." His eyes fell for a moment, then he turned to his troops. "Back to work, lads! I want the flotilla to set sail in an hour. Do your final checks."

As the king spoke, Sir Brouglas and Yagub joined them. Even though they were different species, they hugged like a reunited father and son. Another twinge of jealousy struck at Jab's heart. He and Sanu would never get to reunite with their parents, who'd never see their sons grow up.

Yagub was so similar to Jab and Sanu, a brown squirrel from Qawar who spoke Qawari. He shared their color, species, homeland, language, accent, everything except their age and religion. Seeing Yagub almost felt like a preview of what they'd look like in a few months as teenagers.

Brouglas and Ridgerd looked nothing like Mom and Dad, but these two men were as close as they had to father figures anymore, and both of them were willing to fight and even kill to take Jab's home away.

Maybe Ridgerd wasn't the hero everyone thought he was.

"We'll talk more in my quarters, but we have to change plans. Let's go." Ridgerd's voice snapped Jab out of his thoughts.

Following the colossal hamster, Jab dared to get his hopes up. Maybe the invasion would be canceled. Jab was due for some good news. Walking beside Brouglas, Jab felt the beaver's two books in his coat.

He'd tell him soon. Now wasn't the time.

3

SANU

"Do you think you'd recommend me to the Barkheart Order after I'm knighted?"

"Of course! Though I don't know how much weight my word will carry. They're quite exclusive. I'll ask the good king. You'd make a fine addition to their order. You know you'd have to take seedling's oaths, right?"

"Thank you. When my dad got sick when I was Sanu's age, the Barkhearts took us to their monastery, healed him, and taught me about Ganan, Blest be Him. They're the reason I wanted to be a squire. They do so much good, I just want to be part of it, you know? And besides, Nett becoming a Sapling really inspired me. I already have the combat training from you, so all that's left for me is to become a seedling."

"I'm impressed, Yagub. I hope you don't mind me sitting in the front and cheering the loudest when you accept your acorn."

- Overheard conversation between
Yagub and Sir Brouglas

After entering King Ridgerd's quarters, Sanu understood why the royal hamster spent so much time on deck, mingling with the crew. Before, Sanu assumed the king did it to get the soldiers to like him more, but the king couldn't stand up straight in the cabin, so staying inside must've been annoying.

He had to slouch and bend his knees to fit inside, and it seemed uncomfortable. Sanu couldn't imagine being so tall; he had been jealous of the king's stature, but onboard it didn't seem so useful. Ridgerd pulled a chair over to a table and motioned for the others to do the same.

Sanu, Jab, Yagub, and Sir Brouglas seemed like acorns and two twigs beside a Gnaverwood at this table with the hamster king.

"What's the news, King Ridgerd?" Sanu asked.

Jab's eyes widened, so Sanu waved a paw, trying to silently say, "don't worry, me and the king are friends." But as he made the motion, he remembered that this king intended to conquer their home, which would be a damper on any friendship.

Yagub elbowed Sanu and whispered in Qawari, "Don't upset him."

"You have me at a disadvantage, Yagub," the king said. "I'm the only one here who doesn't know your language, now that Sir Brouglas educated himself. I've only got a few phrases, but I didn't learn that one yet."

Covering Yagub's embarrassment, Brouglas gestured a paw toward the squirrels. "I had three fine teachers, my king, not to mention the translation dictionary I'm going to give to Jab. I am sure they would pass on the knowledge."

Ridgerd shook his head. "I'll need them for map correction and translating my eventual messages to Nasalid more than tutoring me."

"What will you say to him?" Jab asked.

Sanu wanted to congratulate his brother for his good phrasing—Jab was newer to the Frenglese language by a few weeks, and he didn't realize how fast Sanu was learning. But this wasn't a good time for that.

"I'm not sure yet," the king replied. "I received an update from Freng, and it contained two pieces of news."

Sanu wanted to focus, but he was drawn to the scant decorations in the room—a nice copy of the Ganandeeds book by the bed, a gold statue of the Ganan's Rake symbol, molded so it could fit in a paw, and a change of clothes beside his armor and swords, hanging up neatly on the wall. A single shelf held a folded-up board for the double siege game. Sanu and the king were due for a rematch.

Sanu's whiskers stiffened—he wasn't paying attention while the king was saying something important.

"So the realm isn't flourishing as I'd hoped while my brother watches the throne," Ridgerd said through a sigh. "I had specifically told him to lower the taxes in my absence since so many rodents left to fight, but he hasn't yet. His letter vaguely said there's been a disturbance." He ran a paw through his hair and looked at Sanu and Jab. "I wish my brother and I were more like the two of you. You get along and understand each other."

Sanu and Jab exchanged an awkward glance. Sometimes his twin felt like a stranger wearing Sanu's face, and yet he was the only family Sanu had left. He couldn't stop himself from sabotaging their relationship. That didn't feel like understanding each other.

"What else did the prince's letter say?" Brouglas asked, and Sanu wished he could give him some cheese for taking the focus off Sanu and Jab.

The king's ears twitched. "I wasn't the only one who set out for the holy island. King Rattarossa set sail for Qawar with his own army."

"I thought he was an emperor?" Yagub asked.

Brouglas's eyes widened, and he shook his head so fast it resembled a shiver.

Ridgerd's frown melted into a scowl. "That blowhard dormouse calls himself that, but there is no true emperor in the Great Sea. He's a king of an island, just like me."

"S-sorry, my king," Yagub stammered.

"But this is good," Brouglas said. "The two of you will have a force too big for Nasalid to resist. He'll surrender without a fight."

"Rattarossa thinks he's an emperor. His plan wouldn't be liberating one city and restoring the old status quo." Ridgerd's voice darkened and Sanu's blood chilled. "He wants to conquer Qawar. He won't sign a peace with Nasalid—he'll put his head on a spear and display it at the Holy City."

Kill Nasalid? Sanu's heart thumped so hard he worried the others would hear.

Jab shook his head. "I spent time with Nasalid, King Ridgerd. He is a—" He nudged Sanu and changed languages. "—Sanu, how do you say 'brilliant tactician' in Frenglese?"

Before Sanu could answer, Yagub spoke. "Jab said Nasalid is a master strategist."

A smirk crawled up Ridgerd's snout. "Then this will be a great test."

Great?

The king was excited to fight, and Sanu couldn't believe his surprise. He'd suspected persuading Ridgerd out of violence would be impossible, but now he'd have to convince two foreign kings not to destroy their home.

Sanu had been praying more in the last few months, but nothing compared to the cry of his heart in that moment. He couldn't let war come back to Qawar, and he and Jab would do anything to stop it.

Hoping their twin connection would do its magic, Sanu gazed at Jab. With his eyes and ear twitches, Sanu tried to tell him, "We have to stop him," and Jab nodded back grimly.

"Rattarossa's arrival ahead of ours means we need to change our sailing plans," Ridgerd said. "We'll make port near Kraksnout Castle. Rattarossa will reclaim that stronghold first. He's bringing a contingent of the Barkheart Order knights with him. While we're sailing, you will all examine my maps so we'll know where to strike and reinforce."

Images of Sanu's hometown burning raced through his mind.

4

JAB

On the week of Forgiveness Festival, Ganan came across a field where slaves toiled, and He demanded to see the chief farmer. Ganan asked when the workers last had a break or received pay, and the farmer spat on the ground. Ganan knelt in the dirt, dug his paws into the soil, and all the stalks of grain fell, as if cut by the wind. He then bowed his head to the farmer. "You have your grain. Pay these rodents a living wage, allow them food and water while they work, and remember no rodent is property. If you do not, expect the All-Planter to cut you down on Pruning Day as I have done to your crops." The farmer dropped to the ground and begged for forgiveness, and Ganan replied, "How much you are forgiven will match how kind you are in the rest of your days."

- Excerpt from the Ganandeeds,
"The Farmer."

Jab winced at the map sprawled in front of him. It wasn't quite right, and not just because of the misspelled location names. The map read "The Holy Island," which was not the right name. This was Qawar, Jab's home. Its coastline was too jagged in some places and too smooth in others. The lone correct detail was the grand Gnaverwood, the olive tree so tall it acted like a sundial for the whole island. Other islands had Gnaverwoods, but none quite like theirs.

On the parchment map, the metropolis of ZelZaytun ringed the tree, though on Ridgerd's map, it was given its false name preferred by the Sprouters: Olihort. Roads that were a little too straight branched out from the city, connecting to the ports around the island. One cut through Rattin, and Jab had to suppress a chuckle over how it was labeled "Rat-towne." He wished "Olihort" was just a translation mistake or a misheard name and not the attempt to erase a cultural identity.

South of ZelZaytun was a crudely drawn spot—a tree-rimmed lake, with a fishing boat drawn on it, and a little symbol: Ganan's Rake. That small scratch of lines brought a memory that seared Jab's mind, and a shadow fell over the symbol, just like Nasalid's raiders had colored the supply depot there with blood.

Jab's first battle still replayed in his nightmares. The screams. The fire. The crunches of steel and bone.

"Jab?" Sanu's voice snapped him out of the darkness, thank the All-Planter.

The shadow over the symbol was cast by King Ridgerd's finger. "Was this the spot, lad?"

"Um," Jab stuttered, his mouth suddenly dry. "I'm sorry, what?"

Sir Brouglas placed a paw on Jab's shoulder. "It was, my king. Nasalid took that supply depot before his attack on the main city."

Jab appreciated how the beaver didn't call it by its Sprouter name. "I was there," Jab rasped. "I watched the depot get taken over." Jab noticed Sanu's jaw drop.

Ridgerd's tone softened. "I see. My question dredged up foul memories. I'm sorry. I won't make you accompany me there when we take it back."

Jab's heart leapt to his throat as the thought of more death bubbled in his mind.

After whispering "Do you know what 'dredged' means?" to Jab, Sanu inched toward the edge of his seat. "But King Ridgerd, I thought you wanted to negotiate with Nasalid."

The king sighed. "I do. In my prayers, I beg the All-Planter for many things. That is one of them. In my experience, though, the most common answer to my prayers appears to be a 'no' from the Almighty." A far-off look clouded Ridgerd's eyes, and Jab wondered what the king thought.

Brouglas turned to Jab and Sanu. "A good king and good general both require backup plans. We hope for the best and prepare for the worst." He leaned over and winked at Yagub. "A good knight does too."

Ridgerd eyed the twins. "I know your loyalties are conflicted. You do not wish for your home to be engulfed in the flames of war. But you must understand, every ship in this fleet is full of soldiers like me, all of whom believe we will be granted access to the Walled Garden when we die. The price of abandoning this pilgrimage, in many of their eyes, is an eternity in the Droughtlands. I must get them to the sacred city. You must understand how important this is."

Jab lowered his head and found his voice. "My grandparents were killed with all the other Grovekeepers in the city when your grandfather conquered it. Nasalid reclaimed the city for us, and he forgave everyone instead of killing them."

The beaver knight and squirrel squire nodded. "We wouldn't be here if it weren't for that jird's generosity," Brouglas said. "I would remind my king that he did welcome all Sprouter pilgrims to visit the city without weapons. Jab has a good point."

Ridgerd slid out of his chair and crouch-walked to a mostly-empty shelf near his bed and grabbed a box that looked like it held a double siege set. The king returned to his chair, opened the box, and began removing the game pieces individually. He pulled out the red general piece and placed it on the map over ZelZaytun, but not directly on the drawing of the tree. Jab's eyes unfocused, and he realized the tree was drawn in the shape of Ganan's Rake. It was an impressive stylistic art choice, even if it wasn't entirely accurate.

"This is Nasalid," Ridgerd said, indicating the general piece. He withdrew the blue general piece and placed it over a castle in the island's corner, which Jab assumed was Kraksnout Castle, the fortress built by the invaders fifty years ago. "And this is King Rattarossa. This dormouse will occupy this castle and use it as his base. I can't know what's in his heart, but I doubt he prays for the same peace I do. As long as he lives and has the Barkheart Order supporting him with prayers and knights, he will turn the sands red with Grovekeeper blood. You were at Phranktonbourg, Brouglas. You know I'm right."

A dark expression came over the beaver's eyes, but Sanu was busy mumbling, "It's not a desert island. There's plenty of grass and trees."

Yagub elbowed him. "Don't talk to the king that way."

"He's right though," Brouglas said, voice heavy. "You don't know what we saw at Phranktonbourg."

"Nor should they. It was horrific." Ridgerd waved a paw and examined the red vanguard piece. "Yagub, I hope Sanu continues to talk to me that way. As he'll tell you, I'm 'not his king.' I need you all to fill in my knowledge gaps. Now, Jab, I understand you were in Nasalid's scout corps. Where was his forward base before he besieged Olihort?"

Jab's eyes widened. "I-I'm n-not sure." His heart raced. He wouldn't betray the Liberator.

Under the table, Sanu's tail brushed against Jab's, as if to say either, "Good job" or "Don't ruin this."

"He only gave his scouts partial information?" Ridgerd asked. "I suppose that's wise in case a scout is captured. Well, we know he attacked the lake depot—" He placed one of the vanguard pieces over it. "—and we know about the Battle at the Horns of Rat-towne." He placed the second red vanguard piece over the poorly-rendered Rattin, where two curled horns were drawn just to the north of it.

The sketch was ridiculous, since the rocky outcroppings everyone called "horns" much more resembled cones. Still, hearing about the battle there reminded Jab of when he and Sanu were separated and set off on this crazy adventure.

Brouglas pointed in between the two pieces. "His camp must've been somewhere near here. My guess would be a little closer to the trees for protection."

It took everything in Jab's power to avoid blurting out that Brouglas was correct. This flawed map might be the only thing that would stop the king from making a bloody swath across Qawar.

But not correcting the details would mean the death of thousands of soldiers, most of whom were deeply religious rodents who believed this fight would give them a second chance. Jab's heart sank. He didn't want anyone to die. There had to be another way.

5

SANU

We couldn't save ZelYorbua in time. The lieutenants talk about the stench of the place, I think, because they're terrified of what we saw. I shudder to remember it myself, but I know two things for certain, the atrocity was done by the Knights of the Barkheart Order, and I revisit that place in my nightmares.

— Diaries of General Ironseed's secretary

Cheers erupted from outside, and Sanu was relieved the focus left the map.

"What's going on?" King Ridgerd asked.

Gasping, Yagub rushed to the porthole. "The holy tree! The sacred Gnaverwood!"

Sanu's heart raced and he studied his brother's drooped whiskers. For so long, Jab had refused to gaze upon the holy olive tree, out of the tradition that Grovekeepers would avert their eyes from it while the invaders from Freng held the Holy City. They'd looked at it together for the first time after Nasalid liberated the city. The thought of having to block it from their vision again felt like a rock in Sanu's stomach, and he knew it hurt Jab even more.

"The wind must have been on our side," the king said. "We arrived faster than what the captain promised."

Yagub glanced over his shoulder at the king. "It's because the All-Planter is on our side!"

Sanu's eyes narrowed. Yagub seemed to forget that *he* was Qawari also.

"I think it's because we redirected the course toward the point where Castle Kraksnout is, my liege," Brouglas said in a more neutral tone.

"Come on, lads, let's see how much longer until we make landfall." The royal hamster left the cabin with Yagub and Brouglas following.

Jab grabbed Sanu's wrist, preventing him doing the same.

Brouglas held open the door and arched an eyebrow. "Aren't you joining us? You can't stay in the king's quarters alone."

Sanu knew how much it hurt Jab to lie, so he made eye contact with the kind beaver. "I asked Jab if we could pray together once we saw the sacred tree again. Is that all right, since he hasn't taken the Sprouter oaths yet?"

The beaver cracked a smile. "Pray in any language and style you choose, boys. The All-Planter is also an All-Hearer and All-Knower. Your prayers will find their destination." He stepped outside.

Sanu sighed. He hated himself for telling a lie, especially to someone so sincere. But the brothers needed to plan, and their goal was to save lives. Not to mention this would mean Jab wouldn't have to lie again.

"I hope my habit of telling lies isn't rubbing off on you," Jab said. "What can we do to end the fighting before it starts?"

"You know Nasalid better than me," Sanu said. "Do you think he'd let Ridgerd take the city?"

Jab's eyes lowered. "I don't particularly think he *should*. Nasalid didn't make himself a king and take the old throne in the city for himself. He has a Mulcher, a Grovekeeper, and a certain Sprouter you have a crush on running the city together."

Sanu's cheeks flushed. "She's not just anybody, she's a Sapling. But that doesn't change how nobody outside Qawar sees it that way."

Jab placed a finger to his lips. "Ridgerd is the one who needs to stand down and back off. He helped the rodents on Coppergrass, but that's not a reason to let him bring an army to our home."

Sanu's embarrassment melted into frustration. "We're past the point of letting him do anything. He has an army and he's going to use it."

What a pellet eater.

Jab winced. "I'm sorry. We keep promising each other we won't fight, and here I was ready to call you a name. We can both agree we don't want anyone to fight, but we've got two strong generals, three if you count that Rassarotta guy, and they are all willing to die for their beliefs."

"Rattarossa," Sanu corrected. "Sorry. But Ridgerd is really persuasive. He got a whole ship of soldiers who mutinied against him to un-mutiny and join back up."

Whiskers stiffening, Jab leaned forward. "Ridgerd should not persuade Nasalid to do anything." He closed his eyes, relaxed his shoulders, and inhaled. "But he could maybe persuade people back in Freng to give up the fight. If Nasalid and Ridgerd meet, Ridgerd could see for himself that Nasalid is noble and a rodent of his word. And he'd have to start with this Rattarossa guy."

"That's a good plan," Sanu said. "Let's get Brouglas on our side. Everyone trusts him. He can go with us to Nasalid, and then we'll get Nasalid to meet up with Ridgerd away from Rattarossa."

The cheering outside grew to a fever pitch. "We've been a few minutes," Sanu said. "We should go so nobody gets suspicious. Do you want me to help you tell Brouglas you aren't taking the Sprouter oaths?"

Jab rose from his chair, but didn't make eye contact. "Do you think he'll still go along with our plan if he knows the truth? Ridgerd won't let us go to Nasalid without a knight protecting us, and the only one we trust is Brouglas."

Sanu smirked. "I've got some news for you: Ridgerd isn't our king."

Jab chuckled and approached the door. "I suppose you're right. I'd appreciate you being with me. I hope he's not mad."

Sanu opened the door and motioned for Jab to leave first. Yagub was waiting outside for them.

"The king ordered everyone to rest up," Yagub said. "Big day tomorrow."

"What do you mean?" Sanu asked, shielding his eyes from the harsh sun.

Yagub pointed to the crow's nest above them. "The spotter saw Castle Kraksnout's towers with the spyglass. He saw Emperor Rattarossa's flags."

"So what's the hurry?" Jab asked.

Yagub's voice fell. "He also saw siege engines around it. Nasalid's forces are already there and attacking the castle. We're joining the fight tomorrow."

Tense sailors and soldiers left the edge of the sailing cog, brushing past Sanu like he wasn't there. They moved in a throng, anticipating an attack on Sanu's countryrodents.

When the soldiers cleared, Sanu stumbled toward the ship's edge, leaning over the railing. The grand Gnaverwood rose in the distance, and a smaller gray bump appeared to its left.

Sanu's lip trembled. The colossal tree should've been a beautiful sight to behold, but from here, it more closely resembled a paw, reaching out, begging for help.

6

JAB

Seeing Prince Ridgerd in action at Phranktonbourg opened my eyes to the nobility of a true warrior. He did not enjoy the fighting even though he excelled at it. We did not cross paths directly, but seeing a young man risk his life for strangers inspired me to do the same. I hope one day I can protect someone the same way he did. Only with the strength and assistance of Ganan, Blest be Him, could I do this. And yet as I write, I have to question if that feeling comes from being inspired by the prince or feeling like I'm a failed brother.

- From the prayer journal of Sir Brouglas

Jab finished his prayer with the rising sun as soldiers stomped to the main deck.
They'd make landfall in minutes.

Jab inhaled deeply and gazed at his brother, who had just finished the same prayer. Sanu never used to pray on his own. Maybe he really *had* changed. "I'll confess to Sir Brouglas, then we'll ask him to accompany us to Nasalid."

"Agreed," Sanu said, flashing a kind smile. "He'll understand."

Jab wasn't sure if he meant Brouglas or Nasalid, but he hoped it would be true about both. The soldiers cheered, and King Ridgerd strode to the ship's prow and held his sword aloft.

"Our brothers from Rotteland are pinched in by the enemy. We'll come at them from the side, wreck their engines, and make them rue the day. For Olihort!"

The soldiers and sailors raised spears, swords, and devilbeaks aloft, chanting, "For Olihort!"

A lone knight kept his weapon at his side.

Sir Brouglas, beaver knight.

Jab waved Sanu over, and they meandered through the crowd to reach him. Hearing the Sprouter name for the Holy City grated on Jab's ears, but he had to ignore the insult. This was for ZelZaytun. He grabbed the beaver's paw, catching his attention.

Sir Brouglas glanced down at them over his shoulder and signaled to move over to the opposite side of the boat—it looked like he'd wanted to talk too.

When they parted from the crowd, Jab breathed deep and met the knight's eyes. "I wanted to give your holy books and translation guide back."

"Read them already?" he asked with a chuckle.

Jab shook his head and tried to keep his nausea in check. "Back on Coppergrass, I lied about taking the Sprouter oaths. That was the only way they'd let me out of that dungeon."

The beaver leaned back, whiskers drooping. "I see."

The first threat of tears formed on Jab's eyelids. "I'm so sorry. I did mean the other things though. You showed me kindness that I never thought a Sprouter could have. I still see you as a role model of faith, even... even if I ... don't believe the same things." Jab winced, reaching into his coat, producing the two books.

Brouglas sighed. "How about as an apology, you read them anyway? The stories are beautiful. The All-Planter's most precious gift to us is our lives, and we only get one. I'm not mad you lied to save your life, especially since the two of you managed to save King Ridgerd's reputation and Coppergrass Isle in the process. Thank you for telling the truth. I know that must have been hard."

Jab's eyes sank to his hindpaws. Some part of him would've preferred getting yelled at to forgiveness. Now he *had* to read them.

Sanu rested a paw on Jab's shoulder. "Sir Brouglas, there was something else we wanted to talk about."

The beaver surveyed the approaching land, possibly counting the catapults. "We don't have much time."

"We know," Sanu said. "We want to ask Nasalid to meet with Ridgerd. You know Ridgerd is reasonable, and Jab knows that Nasalid is too."

In other circumstances, Jab would've said that he could speak for himself, but he appreciated what Sanu was doing. "Yes," Jab said, finding his squeak of a voice. "You were there when Nasalid said he wanted the feud to end. You carried a copy of his message. You know that he and Ridgerd can work something out, and Ridgerd can persuade everyone in Freng to give up attacking ZelZaytun."

Brouglas faced Castle Kraksnout. "Rattarossa will be a problem, lads. I know him by reputation. His forces were at Phranktonbourg too. He is a cold and fierce dormouse. I'll collect Yagub, and we'll get the messenger's flag."

Behind them, the soldiers dispersed, prepping rowboats and affixing their armor. King Ridgerd, already covered in plate mail, marched over to them, holding a steel helmet with a crown molded into it.

"There are my twin cartographers," the hamster said. "You'll stay on the ship. I won't have an arrow going through either of your skulls."

Jab breathed deep. "No. We'll go to Nasalid's camp and speak with him."

The king folded his arms over his chest and looked at Sanu, letting his helmet dangle by a finger. "I suppose I have *you* to thank for this remark? Did you say 'he's not our king' to him?"

Brouglas stepped between them. "My liege, I will protect them. Under the messenger's flag, no harm will come to them. You can still commence the counter siege, and we will go meet in your name. What message would you have us give to Nasalid?"

The king placed his helmet on his head, making him seem even taller. "Tell him I will meet with him snout-to-snout. We will work this out like civilized rodents."

Jab eyed the giant sword strapped to Ridgerd's back. He thought it was called a "claymore," but he'd need to double check with Sanu. Nothing about that weapon seemed civilized, even less so with the helmet muffling Ridgerd's voice.

"So you'll let us go?" Jab asked.

"You three may," the king replied. "But Brouglas, I'm keeping your squire aboard the ship. If this mission fails, I'm losing too many potential translators. Come back to me with good news." He rubbed a smudge on his helmet. "I suppose this will be somewhat of a race. Get the message to him before I break through this siege and liberate Rattarossa's troops."

The ships were close enough that shouts from the shore carried over. Images of past battles threatened at the edge of Jab's mind, but he wouldn't let those haunt him or keep him from acting. Not when he needed to run toward peace.

7

SANU

"I saw that giant king mow down ten enemies with one sword strike."

"I heard he took a crossbow bolt to the shoulder and it bounced off him."

"Somebody in the other unit said he once defeated an assassin with nothing but a trumpet."

"I can't believe anyone ever doubted him. Long live good King Ridgerd!"

— Overheard chatter in the ranks of soldiers

Sanu ran alongside Jab and Brouglas, who carried the red flag with a white tooth design denoting a messenger. Sanu had equipped Dad's scimitar to his belt and Jab did the same with the light crossbow he'd earned in his time with Nasalid's scout corps, and the beaver knight carried a war axe on his back and Ridgerd's rolled-up message on his hip.

The trio banked to the right, hugging the beach, and Ridgerd stormed forward, dashing Sanu's vain hope that he'd help Nasalid instead of this other guy's fighters.

Metal clanged on metal as soldiers wailed.

It would be a bloody day.

The battered flags flying atop Kraksnout Castle shared the symbol of a crowned bear, which Sanu understood belonged to King Rattarossa, based on the soldiers' chatter aboard the sailing cog. Behind the flagship, the other troop transports disembarked their soldiers, and the counter siege began in earnest, though Sanu wondered if Ridgerd could break the fight single-pawed.

Sanu had visited Kraksnout with Brouglas back before Nasalid's liberation of ZelZaytun, and it had been to empty the garrison and protect the Holy City ahead of Nasalid's attack, but due to some treachery on the part of Nasalid's former adviser, the garrison was incapacitated.

How many of those soldiers had belonged to this Barkheart Order? As the three of them ran along the beach, Sanu lost count of how many catapults ringed the castle, and wondered how many of those had been used only months before to ransack the outer walls of the Holy City.

After a few minutes, a jerboa on horseback rode out to them, wielding a scimitar. Emblazoned on his leather breastplate was the double-wolf sigil, the sign of Nasalid the Liberator.

The jerboa turned his horse to the side, held out a paw, and spoke in Frenglese. "What kind of messenger comes at the same time as an attacking force?" He shifted his gaze to Sanu and Jab and spoke Qawari. "Boys, what are you doing with him? Are you prisoners? Or have you forgotten Qawar and become Freng rats?"

"Rats?" Brouglas seethed.

Jab stepped forward and removed his crossbow from his hip. "I was in the Liberator's scout corps. I, my brother, and this knight, were part of Nasalid's delegation to the Frenglese kings. We were unable to return any faster. One of the Frenglese kings brought us here. He wishes to meet with Nasalid."

The jerboa scoffed and pointed at the battle raging in the distance. "Is he hoping to meet him at sword point? The Freng kings are the least of our worries since this invader from Rotteland came."

"Will you take us to Nasalid?" Brouglas asked. "We could not get King Ridgerd to call off the attack, but once he has a stronghold here, he will believe himself to be in a better spot to negotiate."

The stench of smoke smacked Sanu's nostrils and he watched as a catapult burned. "Do you want that to happen to ZelZaytun?" Sanu asked. "Take us to Nasalid."

"The Liberator isn't here," the jerboa said. "I will take you to my commanding officer. He'll decide what to do with you."

The clang of steel against iron intensified, as did the acrid smoke fumes. Jab looked pale, as if he relived something awful, probably that battle at the lake.

The jerboa motioned for them to follow him and he nudged his horse around.

Sanu tapped Jab's shoulder with his bushy tail. "Hey. We're safe. That fire won't hurt us."

Jab nodded, and the far-off stare faded. "I know. Thank you."

They followed the jerboa back to camp, where gerbils, squirrels, and jerboas scrambled to suit up in armor and grab scimitars, maces, and spears, and ride toward the battle. A burly gerbil barked out orders, and Sanu noticed the two falcon feathers on his helmet, denoting his rank.

The jerboa dismounted in front of the gerbil. "Serenity to your family, sir. I have messengers from the Frenglese king who just landed. They claim to have ties to the Liberator."

The gerbil squinted and glared at Sanu and Jab, and after a half-second, his eyes widened. "Tranquility to your home. Ah, the hero twins. We all thought you'd died."

Sanu found the title of "hero" to be awesome and horrifying in equal measure.

The jerboa stared at his hindpaws. "I'm sorry, sir, I thought everyone said the twins were jirds, not squirrels."

Shaking his head, the gerbil replied, "You dolt. There are five jirds in the whole army, and two of them are Nasalid and his brother." Exhaling and addressing Sanu and Jab, he softened his tone. "Serenity to your family, boys. I will hear this message for the Liberator. Make it—"

Distant cheers rang out from the battlefield. Sanu whipped around before he had a chance to reply with "tranquility to your home." The towering catapults had all fallen, and the other soldiers remaining in the camp froze.

"We were too slow," Jab muttered.

A ragged and bloody squirrel limped toward them. "Sir!" he shouted to the commander. "We're overrun. They charged like they were fleeing the Droughtlands. We didn't stand a chance."

"How many are dead?" the officer demanded.

The squirrel hung his head. "I don't know, sir. But I saw whole squadrons taken inside the castle as prisoners, and that was before the last catapult fell."

"Prisoners," the officer muttered.

Sanu's mouth dried. He got a better appreciation for why the king made decisions from the front—this officer was dealing with information that was already minutes old, a catastrophic loss of time in a battle. He also understood why Nasalid didn't show up to battles in person.

Sir Brouglas faced the officer and waved his rolled-up parchment with the king's message. "Perhaps you can meet with King Ridgerd yourself. The fact he took prisoners is proof he wants to negotiate."

But they didn't have that same guarantee from King Rattarossa.

8

JAB

Along Ganan's way to the Holy City for the Festival of Fallen Kings, Ganan came across a commune of rodents cursed with rabies. With cracked lips, they muttered nonsense and attacked anyone who approached. Ganan's followers begged Him to keep walking, but Ganan approached the rabid rodents. Ganan drew a circle in the dirt around Himself with His rake, stood at the center, and invited the rabid ones to embrace Him. They shambled forward, but when they crossed the circle, color returned to their lips, their speech returned, and Ganan hugged them. They drank water and returned home.

- Excerpt from the Ganandeeds, "The Circle."

Jab marched toward Kraksnout Castle, a place historians compared to a stronghold of the Droughtlands itself. Soldiers in Nasalid's camp once chuckled about how foolish it was for the garrison here to be emptied. Jab wondered what they'd say about Nasalid's siege engines lying broken and burning around its ramparts.

Under the safety of Brouglas's messenger banner, Jab, Sanu, and the commanding officer—a gerbil named Ayrim—marched toward the castle's outer gate, passing by Grovekeeper troops stripping off their armor and dropping their weapons. Their mutters reached Jab's ears.

"I got a smack at his armor and my mace bounced off."

"He blunted my spear's point. The metal crumpled like paper against him."

"My friend dove on his back to try and shake him off, and the war king flung him like a gnat."

Jab's fur stood on end. They were discussing King Ridgerd.

One phrase moved through the group of prisoners more than their body odor. "Steel fur."

People were saying Ridgerd himself had fur made of steel. It sounded so ridiculous, but overhearing the snippets made Jab question what kind of warrior Ridgerd truly was. Maybe he *had* done all those things on Coppergrass that Sanu claimed and more. He didn't want to match those feats against Nasalid, not for one second.

They climbed a hill toward the next set of castle walls. The fortress proper stood so far away that Jab understood why Nasalid's catapults didn't have the same effect as on the Holy City. Jab's muscles burned, making him wonder if he would've been strong enough to climb this much a year ago.

The castle gates opened, and soldiers greeted Brouglas with cheers. A dormouse patted him on the back and said something that didn't sound like Frenglese.

"What did he say?" Jab whispered to Sanu.

Sanu furrowed his brow. "I... don't know."

Brouglas glanced over his shoulder. "He spoke Rottelander. He's one of King Rattarossa's rodents. I fought beside him at Phranktonbourg."

"Rottelander?" Jab asked.

"It's what they speak in Rotteland," Ayrim said, adjusting his officer's hat. "My dad was a trader and taught me a bit about the place. It's like Freng but with better food and worse manners."

"Better food and worse manners?" Brouglas chuckled. "Add stronger berry juice and you've described it perfectly."

Ayrim scowled, curling his skinny tail. "Grovekeepers don't drink berry juice, you Freng swine. It's poison."

"He's not a pig," Jab said. "He's one of the good Sprouters."

Brouglas smiled, facing forward.

As they strode up the hill, Jab peeked around the open hillside, trying to count the prisoners of war. It seemed like the prisoners outnumbered the dead, which wasn't much consolation. The sheer number of captured soldiers was staggering.

Jab tried to estimate, but there were hundreds, probably more. He couldn't imagine what kind of blow that would be to Nasalid's numbers. A counterattack would be risky, maybe pointless.

Ridgerd was starting these negotiations with an upper paw before they'd agreed to them.

Changing details on Ridgerd's map wouldn't have even mattered. The ultimate invader castle was now in the paws of the ultimate warrior.

They reached the second layer of walls at the hilltop, and the gates clanked open to cheers from the garrisoned soldiers.

Jab noticed what was on each of their suits of armor, a stitched bear's head wearing a crown with a Ganan's Rake design, emblazoned on a shield.

"That's King Rattarossa's symbol?" Jab asked.

"Aye," Ayrim replied. "That dormouse has a reputation like a bear too."

The soldiers manning the gate escorted Jab, Sanu, Brouglas, and Ayrim inside the central keep. The portcullis didn't open as wide as Jab would've guessed. As big as the castle was on the outside, the inside was cramped. An arched hallway opened into a larger atrium, with a grand map table in the center. Standing at it was a hunched-over King Ridgerd, still in armor, and a barrel-chested dormouse. This dormouse had a rake-themed crown matching his bear symbol, which sat atop a shock of red fur that framed his face like a lion's mane, and a matching beard reached down to his heart. His black eyes stood out in contrast with his red fur. His flowing cape was cut into a deep V, and his muscles strained against his leather armor. He didn't match Ridgerd's height, but he did match his commanding presence.

Sir Brouglas bowed to Ridgerd. "My liege." Then he did the same to the dormouse. "King Rattarossa, it is a pleasure to meet you."

"*King*?" The dormouse stepped away from the table. His accent was thick enough that Jab wasn't confident he understood. "You would do well to call me by my proper title." He shot a glare at a lemming standing by the wall. "Do your job."

The lemming tightly nodded and stepped forward. "You all stand in the presence of Emperor Rattarossa, crowned by the Arborist, protector of Holy Rotteland."

King Ridgerd rolled his eyes. "I told you before, we aren't grandstanding. Look, they've brought the commanding officer."

Rattarossa harrumphed. "My crown was placed between my ears by the Arborist. Rotteland is the center of the Great Sea. You will bend the knee to me, Ridgerd."

The hamster sauntered over to the dormouse and leaned over him. "You'll have to excuse me, but my knee is a bit stiff from running around these grounds and saving your tail." He sighed and turned to Jab and Sanu. "Now, what have my fine informants brought to me?"

"Informants?" Ayrim hissed in Qawari.

"That's not really true," Jab whispered back.

Sanu cleared his throat. "King Ridgerd, we were about to deliver your message to be sent to Nasalid when we got news of your victory here."

Jab wouldn't call hundreds of captured Grovekeepers a "victory," but now wasn't the time to argue.

"You sent a message?" Rattarossa asked, stroking his red beard. "Seeking a separate peace with the enemy?"

"My message was a simple command," Ridgerd replied. He eyed the commanding officer. "Where is Nasalid? I will speak with him."

The officer spat on the floor. "He's in the Droughtlands. How about you two go there and look for him?"

Rattarossa clapped his paws. "Ha! I like this one." He turned to the lemming who'd announced him and chortled something in Rottelander.

Ridgerd rounded the table and leaned against it, lowering his head to lock eyes with the officer. "I've heard tales of Nasalid's generosity. I am sure when his time does come, the All-Planter will welcome him into the Walled Garden. I will speak plainly. We will exchange the prisoners here for the surrender of Olihort."

"It's 'ZelZaytun,' you pellet sniffer," Ayrim snapped. "Do you have any updates on your trip to the Droughtlands? The ocean is nearby. Jump in with your armor on and you'll get there very fast."

Jab's eyes widened, and he nudged Sanu. Sanu stepped between the officer and the king. "Don't talk to him like that. The king is reasonable."

Jab would've said "dangerous," but now probably wasn't the time.

"Fine," the officer said. "You wish me to convey your message to Nasalid? You'll let me go back to him?"

"No," Rattarossa said. "You will summon Nasalid to us. We can't trust you, since you're willing to call little Ridgerd a 'pellet sniffer.'" The dormouse leaned forward and with a theatrical gesture, brough his paw to the side of his snout and fake whispered, "though you should hear the other names he's called."

Ridgerd glared at Rattarossa. "*No*, we will find a neutral place to meet."

"He'll murder you," Rattarossa taunted. "So you know what, go ahead. Your brother will make a fine vassal in the Holy Rotteland Empire. He's not as strong-willed as you, if I remember your father's complaints about you two correctly. He'll gladly accept my reign in exchange for your throne; he'll make a fine puppet in my grand empire."

Ridgerd ground his teeth with enough force that it gave Jab a toothache.

"We'll accompany you and this officer," Jab said. "Nasalid trusts us."

"No more." Ridgerd threw a look like a dagger at Rattarossa. "How about we end the day's bickering and celebrate our victory? We'll get an accurate count of our casualties and prisoners, then we can send Nasalid a formal message from both of us?"

"I'm not feeding three thousand prisoners," Rattarossa said.

"It'll come from my supplies," Ridgerd said.

The dormouse cracked a toothy smile. "Fine."

Jab measured the dormouse. He'd seen brutal warriors who enjoyed killing, and conniving politicians who would do anything to remove their rivals. In King Rattarossa, he saw both.

9

SANU

A cousin of mine is a Sprouter, and I asked him about the Barkheart Order on General Ironseed's behalf. He said their official role on Qawar was to protect holy sites important to Ganan and provide medical treatment to the wounded. Their numbers swelled with the invasion. I pressed him about the atrocities we saw, and he seemed shocked. He said they'd fight to protect a relic or location, but he insisted that would be the end of it. My cousin is an honest rodent, so I am quite perplexed.

- Diaries of General Ironseed's secretary

Each day in Kraksnout Castle kept Sanu on edge. Anxiety over the unreturned messenger made Sanu worry that he'd been eaten by a hyena or fled the island. Troops grumbled about Ridgerd feeding so many prisoners, despite putting them to work tending the vast land within Kraksnout's walls. Ridgerd's flotilla bobbed offshore, though he sent two ships back to the Freng Islands with news of their success and two others to Rotteland, since Nasalid's fleet had obliterated Rattarossa's the week before the siege.

Listening to the prisoners revealed a deep divide in how they saw either king. The nickname "Ridgerd Steelfur" caught on so fast that some of Ridgerd's own troops started using it. But Rattarossa's nicknames among the prisoners came closer to "Paper Bear," "Lost Bear," and "Pellet Beard." Those failed to spread to the other side.

Both kings argued at each opportunity and couldn't agree what their next move ought to be, so their decision was to send the gerbil officer who'd surrendered back to Nasalid. At Rattarossa's insistence, nobody else was allowed to accompany him.

Word from the Liberator came with a messenger one morning as Sanu and Jab finished their sunrise prayers, as if the All-Planter had answered them immediately.

Ayrim, the surrendered officer, looked worse for wear with patches missing from his fur. Sanu and Jab were allowed to be present when his message was delivered to the kings, because Ridgerd demanded as many translators as possible so no meanings might be lost. Knowing Sir Brouglas, he probably also insisted the boys be there.

Standing in the war room, Sanu wished to be anywhere else, but hoped the message would mean they could leave this cramped encampment.

Beside Ridgerd stood one of his lieutenants, and a Barkheart Order knight stood with Rattarossa. The knight carried a devilbeak on his back, a weapon Sanu had drooled over—a deadly polearm with a spearpoint, a hammer end, and a curved pickax blade. Its shimmery metal construction contrasted against the ring mail which draped over a leather vest, stylized to resemble bark.

Sanu wanted to puzzle out why the armor was made that way, but he didn't want to lose focus on the message.

The gerbil officer-messenger unrolled a scroll and cleared his throat.

"From the secretary of Nasalid, Liberator of Qawar and protector of the Holy Tree, who writes on his behalf."

"His secretary?" Ridgerd scoffed.

"He's insulting us," Rattarossa added.

Ayrim lowered his message and glared at them. "I'm speaking." The gerbil cleared his throat again and raised the message. "It would seem my message to Freng did not arrive. King Ridgerd, I am praying for you as you cope with the loss of your father. And King Rattarossa, I understand you are building an empire. Look elsewhere. I did not send a missive to Rotteland to inform you of the Frenglese invaders surrendering ZelZaytun, since it did not seem to me that it would concern one such as yourself. I did not realize the ties between Sprouter nations were so close. Forgive me if that was perceived as an insult. I understand you have seized the empty Kraksnout Castle and repelled my forces. Ayrim insists you took them prisoner." The gerbil straightened and some spirit returned to his face as he lowered his message again. "I *did* insist that, kings."

Sanu's tail hairs stiffened and his mouth dried, watching the Barkhearts grip their weapons tighter. He sidestepped a fraction closer to Sir Brouglas.

Ayrim raised his message. "I trusted him to lead a force, so I am trusting him again. Know this: Sprouters live in ZelZaytun peacefully with Grovekeepers and Mulchers. I know you have your sights set on the Holy City. You cannot hope to take it. I understand you would not wish to return to Freng or Rotteland empty-pawed. Here is my offer. Release the prisoners to me and in exchange, the Sapling of ZelZaytun will donate sacred relics of Ganan kept in the Holy City that you both may take back home. That will satisfy your pilgrimage and we can avoid bloodshed. If you agree, send an emissary to the halfway point on the road between Kraksnout and ZelZaytun. There we shall have the exchange. I do not wish to spill more Sprouter blood upon Qawar's sand and soil, but if you force me to, I will call upon every rodent here to oppose you. If you agree to lay down your weapons, any number of your soldiers may visit the Holy City as pilgrims. In Qawar, we greet each other by wishing peace and tranquility to the other rodent's home. I would urge you to consider that wish."

Rattarossa glanced at the Barkheart knight, and then at the messenger. "Why couldn't Nasalid come here himself?"

Ayrim rolled up his message with his tail. "It would be dishonorable to meet two rodents he intends to expel from the island." A heavy silence passed, and then he added, "Or kill, if he has to."

Ridgerd shook his head. "He must understand that the city is an object of worship for us."

"He *does* understand," Sanu pointed out. "It's a good offer, King Ridgerd. You should take it."

"Do you remember Nasalid's invitation to visit the city as peaceful pilgrims?" Sir Brouglas asked. "He was sincere."

Jab came to Sanu's side. "We'll go with Ayrim. I know Nasalid. I might be able to convince him to meet with you."

Ridgerd arched an eyebrow. "You *do* know him." Then he turned his gaze to Sanu. "And you know me."

"I'm not riding out with you," Rattarossa said. "It's a trap."

"It's not," Ayrim said, aloof.

Sir Brouglas came forward, head bowed. "King Rattarossa—"

"Emperor," the Barkheart knight interjected.

Brouglas nodded. "Apologies. Emperor Rattarossa, I also met Nasalid. He follows the rules of Grovekeepers closely. He would not lie."

A twinge of guilt plucked at Sanu, and he noticed that comment made Jab stare at his hindpaws.

Ridgerd muttered something to himself, then addressed Ayrim. "Would Nasalid's emissaries be willing to meet closer to here?"

"Yes," Rattarossa said. "Within view of the castle. That way, Nasalid can earn our trust." A hunger glowed in his eyes.

The officer rolled his eyes. "You come out as far as you're willing to go, King Ridgerd. I'll tell the emissaries you've come as far as you could, and they will meet you or let you bake in the harsh Qawar sun."

Brouglas stepped away from the kings and leaned toward Sanu, whispering, "I bet he's fun at parties."

A smile cracked Sanu's face, if only to appease Brouglas. Unease at what would happen to his home overshadowed Sanu's eagerness to leave the confines of the castle and be with Ridgerd again. Even though he wasn't Sanu's king, Ridgerd and Brouglas had been something like father figures for Sanu, or at least occupied the title of role model for him, and he knew Brouglas shared that with Jab, along with Nasalid. If they could get Ridgerd and Nasalid together, they'd certainly find a path to peace.

He hoped.

10

JAB

Lord Ganan, Blest be You, please hear me. Lying in this bed, recovering from these wounds, I have never known my heart to darken so. I had nothing but this journal and my copy of Ganandeeds. I finally had the strength to read more than a few words today. With so many stories of you healing the sick and injured, I am praying not for a miracle, but to find the strength to carry on. Focusing on You dulls my pain. If these injuries claim my life, I beg you to let my brother know I still love him and miss him. Send him a sign.

- From the prayer journal of Sir Brouglas

On their way out of the castle, Jab elbowed Sanu. Brouglas, Ridgerd, and a Barkheart Order knight strode in front, the officer-messenger behind them, one of Ridgerd's banner carriers and trumpeters on either side, and the brothers in the back, as the afterthoughts they were. Nobody seemed to pay attention to Jab's light crossbow on his hip.

Jab remembered rodents in Rattin whispering about the Barkhearts; Jab wasn't sure what exactly made them different from knights like Sir Brouglas, but he could tell there was a difference in their fearsome armor and cold demeanor.

"Psst," Jab whispered under the cover of the iron gate's *racka-click*.

Sanu peered over his shoulder. "Are you thinking what I'm thinking?"

Jab cast an eye at Ridgerd. "I think the king was right. You know him well and I know Nasalid well. But they don't know each other at all, and Rattarossa is throwing everything into chaos." Jab was at first worried they were whispering too loudly, but the Barkheart knight's metal armor clanged so much when he walked, that he felt safe to speak.

Sanu nodded slowly. "So if I go to Nasalid, I could tell him what Ridgerd is thinking. If you stay with Ridgerd, you can do the same."

"I don't want to split up again, but what else can we do?"

They descended the gentler hill leading down from the castle's outer wall. Remnants of the battle lay in piles of burnt scraps and bones. Jab didn't blame Ayrim for his demeanor around the kings earlier.

"This time, it'll be different," Sanu said. "We'll know the other one is alive and we'll know where we are."

"And if the leaders allow us, we can send each other messages," Jab added.

"Yeah, that would be nice." Sanu stared into the distance. "Do you think about Rattin at all?"

"Mostly Mom and Dad. But there are little things I'd like again. Sheltercakes, for one."

"And to see Qala, right?" Sanu asked.

Jab suddenly had a new interest in examining his light crossbow. "Only sometimes." It wasn't his fault she was the most beautiful and intelligent gerbil in their hometown. What was a young squirrel to do?

"I'm just messing with you," Sanu said. "I think about Cladh a lot too. She was really nice to me back when she was working for the old Sapling. Now that she took his place, I doubt she'd have time for me."

"She also might not be interested in a Grovekeeper."

"Hey, stranger things have happened," Sanu replied.

The Barkheart knight called for a halt by thumping his devilbeak into the dirt road.

"We've barely walked at all," King Ridgerd protested. He turned around and pointed over Jab's head, back at Castle Kraksnout. "I can still see rodents on the walls. We're nowhere near halfway."

The knight faced Ridgerd. Under his armor, Jab couldn't even tell what species this knight was, which was unsettling. It was as if the armor and what it represented was more central to this rodent's identity than his species or island of origin. Jab didn't like reducing a rodent's identity to one thing, but the sharp lines and cold attitude only left the image of a moving suit of armor, dedicated to fighting for Sprouterism. Maybe that was why they were called Barkhearts instead of Fleshhearts, although 'Fleshhearts' sounded like something out of a monster story. But the triple curving spikes in a rake pattern on his helmet made him seem like a monster all on his own. Even though Ridgerd was taller than the knight, the knight possessed an intimidating presence.

"We are stopping here," he said in a thick accent that matched Rattarossa's. "The Emperor of Holy Rotteland decreed this would be our spot."

"Emperor," Ridgerd hissed. "I am the king standing in front of you and I am saying we are not far enough."

Ayrim huffed. "If this is as far as you will go, I will get the emissaries and bring them here. Let the kids come with me if you don't believe me. I will return with them unharmed."

"We can go with him," Sanu said.

The royal hamster's head snapped around like a whip, and he glared at Sanu and then the officer. "You are not taking those boys anywhere. They are under my protection."

"Then the beaver can come with me," he replied.

Sir Brouglas bowed. "I'll go, my king."

"Go," Ridgerd sighed, waving his paw.

The officer departed with Brouglas, and Jab turned and peered behind them, noticing more rodents lining Kraksnout's walls.

Jab elbowed Sanu again. "No matter what, when they come back, you go with the officer so you can get to Nasalid."

"I don't like you being around all these Barkheart guys," Sanu said.

"Neither does Ridgerd. I'll stay close to him."

A tense hour passed, and Jab occupied himself by monitoring the number of rodents on Kraksnout's walls. They were far away enough that keeping an exact count was difficult, but it felt like there were many more than there had been over the course of their stay since the counter siege.

The officer returned with Brouglas and a pair of jerboas. Jab didn't recognize them, but the number of falcon feathers in their headwraps proved they were members of Nasalid's inner circle.

King Ridgerd's trumpeter stepped forward and played a brief fanfare. In Frenglese, he said, "You stand before King Ridgerd, the youngest and bravest of all the kings in Freng."

Brouglas and Ayrim translated, and then the gerbil officer turned to Ridgerd. "They wish to repeat the offer of prisoners for relics and your— by the All-Planter, what are you doing?" Gasping, Ayrim pointed up at the castle.

Rodents lined the entire castle wall. It was too far for Jab to catch any detail beyond that, but something in the way the outlines moved was wrong. He realized there were two lines of rodents, and the line in front had more than the one in back.

"What's happening?" Jab asked. Whispers of his training kicked in, and he reached for his crossbow.

The first line of rodents plummeted off the wall's battlements. Shouts and screams carried over, muffled by the distance.

There were hundreds of them.

A number formed in Jab's mind and his heart sank.

Three thousand.

The second line of rodents stepped forward, leaning over the edge of the wall, and stepped backward in unison.

Those first rodents had been pushed, screaming in their fall.

"The prisoners," Sanu whispered.

The two jerboas shouted at Ridgerd, as did the gerbil officer.

"This is treachery," King Ridgerd pleaded. "I was feeding those prisoners with my troops' rations. I wanted to exchange them. You have to believe me!"

Jab's breath caught, and he forgot how to move. Three thousand captured prisoners had just been killed. It must have been Rattarossa's order.

Brouglas tried pleading with the emissaries in Qawari. "This was not his doing! There's another king. *He* did this."

"Save it," the officer shot back. "We know what kind of rodents we're dealing with now."

"Wait!" Sanu sprinted forward, and the Barkheart Order knight turned to block his way.

When Sanu didn't change course, the knight lifted his devilbeak.

Jab remembered how to move, and he took off at a sprint as well. He pulled out his light crossbow, which he'd already loaded. He only had one shot. The devilbeak raced down toward Sanu, and Ridgerd and Brouglas reached for the knight, but they wouldn't get there in time.

Jab aimed mid-stride.

Fhwit!

The bolt sailed toward his brother's attacker, smacking the Barkheart's paw. The bolt bounced off like Jab had expected, but it caused the knight's grip to falter. Sanu spun out of the way, and raced past the rest of Ridgerd's delegation, joining the other side.

Jab breathed hard. His brother was safe, but he couldn't say the same for himself or for Rattarossa's victims. A dark thought rose, and Jab wondered if Ridgerd really had known this would happen. A gifted leader like him was supposed to see the double siege board ten moves ahead.

11

SANU

"I heard Emperor Rattarossa's first conquest was one of the smaller islands in Freng. The local lord had a dispute with the Arborist. The emperor defeated him and got his favor that way."

"Have you been hitting the berry juice? He expanded into Boheem first."

"You're both wrong. He married well and got Toscan at the outset. His brother-in-law is a big deal in the Barkheart Order, and they helped him get Boheem, and then he swallowed that Freng island. Don't forget, he left the kings alive and they swore oaths to him, so that is why we call him Emperor."

- Overheard chatter in the Kraksnout garrison

Down the road from where he ran away from Ridgerd, Sanu took refuge with Ayrim and the two jerboa emissaries. The four of them had run from the massacre, but once out of sight of Kraksnout Castle, they stopped and Sanu doubled over, trying to catch his breath. He'd just watched three thousand Grovekeepers shoved off a castle wall.

Ayrim used his whip of a tail to tap the dirt in front of Sanu. "Calm down. Catch your breath. We're safe now."

The emissary on the left, a bit taller than the other with red-striped headwraps, bowed a bit to meet Sanu's eye level, which made his wide ears shake. "We see you're Qawari. Who are you, son?"

Sanu sighed. "My name is Sanu of Rattin. My brother spent time with Nasalid, and after ZelZaytun was liberated, he and I were sent to the Freng Islands to deliver the news."

The emissary in red stripes straightened. "You and your brother are famous in our ranks. I am Mahar, and like you, I have a twin brother." He pointed to the other jerboa emissary, a bit shorter but with darker fur and blue stripes in his headwraps.

The shorter emissary waved. "Sanu of Rattin, I am Zaqar, of Sqirlib."

"And you know me," the gerbil messenger said, and then his voice soured. "Ayrim, the first lieutenant in Qawar to surrender to the mighty Ridgerd Steelfur. I'm sure I'll be remembered as well as General Ironseed."

"What happened to you in Freng?" Zaqar asked.

Sanu's breathing steadied and he straightened. "We arrived on the big island, I can't remember the name, but the king had just died, and that's how Ridgerd became king. He was the designated heir. Once he heard the news, he got pressured into raising an army to fight Nasalid. After getting sidetracked on Coppergrass Island, we came here. My brother and I never got a chance to report back to Nasalid. I escaped them, hoping you all could take me to him."

Mahar whistled, leaning forward on his long hindpaws. "That's quite the story."

"Neither of you believed me when *I* told you that," Ayrim grumbled.

"On Coppergrass, I spent a lot of time with King Ridgerd," Sanu said. "He's a reasonable rodent, and I think he can be talked out of fighting."

"I don't know how possible that is after what we witnessed," Zaqar said.

Sanu's stomach twisted. He was glad he hadn't been closer to the prisoners when they were killed. But he had spent enough time with them to learn their nicknames for the kings. Their deaths were so senseless and wrong. Sanu knew Ridgerd wouldn't do that, but Rattarossa was another story entirely. So many rodents dead, all for a battle that didn't need to happen.

"Can you still take me to him?" Sanu asked.

Mahar waved a paw. "Come on, let's keep moving. Our camp is close. We need to report to the Liberator anyway. You'll come with us.

And you'll tell us what you know about these Frenglese and Rotteland vermin. They're a disease on Qawar."

Brouglas and King Ridgerd weren't vermin though. Neither was Cladh. Sanu had met so many more good rodents than bad ones.

When they reached the camp, Zaqar, Mahar, and Ayrim took to horseback. The gerbil offered to let Sanu ride with him in the saddle. Sanu hesitated before accepting, since the last time Sanu had ridden in a saddle with another rider was when Brouglas had saved his life.

The camp was bare bones, and not at all the military advance force Sanu had imagined. Only a few attendants were present, and they were packing up the tents and extinguishing the few fires they had built. The jerboa brothers detailed the atrocity, but they didn't specify that it was Rattarossa. They just lumped them all into "Sprouters." And while Sanu wanted to protest that King Ridgerd would never do such a horrible thing, the words couldn't leave his mouth. Ridgerd was still an invader. His power combined with Rattarossa's ruthlessness would turn Qawar to ash.

Ridgerd was his enemy, leaving Sanu to question his respect for him.

From the saddle, Sanu gazed around the Qawari countryside. To his right, sparse grass slowly thickened as it stretched toward ZelZaytun, and to his left, rocky terrain surrendered to Qawar's desert. One thing both sides had in common was the long shadow of the holy

Gnaverwood tree, stretching across the landscape like a great sundial.

"We're a few days' ride from the Holy City," Ayrim said. "Do you know where the invaders will strike next?"

"I have an idea, unfortunately." Sanu had taken this road from Kraksnout to ZelZaytun before with Brouglas and Yagub, so he knew about where they were. "I don't think the invaders will go straight for the Holy City. One of the two kings wants to conquer the whole island and the other only has his sights on ZelZaytun. There's a town near here called Rattin." Seeing other rodents show recognition at his hometown's name felt like a new experience. In his time with the Sprouters and on Coppergrass, nobody seemed to know about it except Brouglas and Yagub. "That town is in danger."

Zaqar pulled his horse away. "I've been to Rattin many times in the last few weeks. I'll go."

"Be careful," Mahar warned. "For all we know, there's going to be a third surprise army landing on the opposite shore."

"He's kidding," Ayrim whispered. "It's all loyal Grovekeepers on the islands neighboring on the other side. Nasalid consolidated power there before coming here."

Sanu nodded, watching Zaqar take the fork in the road toward Rattin, the town where his parents died and where he once believed Jab had died. He'd been so confident that splitting up was the right thing, but neither of them had accounted for the Barkheart knight trying to kill

Sanu to prevent his escape. Maybe he'd done the same to Jab the second Sanu was out of sight.

Sanu would have to pray like Jab and beg the All-Planter for help. Sanu would also have to act like Ridgerd and charge forward, taking his life in his own paws.

Galloping toward the Holy City with Mahar and Ayrim, Sanu wondered how much time they had left before more rodents were tossed off walls or into the fire of battle.

12

JAB

> Lord Ganan addressed the crowd from the town square. "While it is good to love friends, Blest be They who can also love those called enemy and stranger. Because there is only one All-Planter, we must strive to love all rodents, especially those we struggle to love. The orphan, the foreigner, even the prisoner deserves your love, protection, and respect."
>
> - Excerpt from the Ganandeeds, "The Sermon in the Garden"

Two days after Sanu escaped, Jab was finally free to leave as well.

"Free" felt like a bit of a stretch.

With the prisoners gone, Rattarossa and Ridgerd had agreed they should depart, but in different directions for a pincer move on the island; both left a contingent of troops to garrison Kraksnout. King Ridgerd took Jab, Sir

Brouglas, Yagub, and his troops, and they were to march down Qawar's east coast. Despite Jab's pleading, Ridgerd planned to isolate the fishing communities to prevent them from supplying ZelZaytun. And despite Ridgerd's pleading, two Barkheart Order knights joined Ridgerd's host.

At Brouglas's suggestion, Ridgerd agreed to accept them in his group in exchange for Rattarossa making a public promise that no future prisoners would be murdered and that they would storm ZelZaytun together once the city was cut off from supplies.

Yagub barely spoke, which Brouglas explained to Jab was a result of him missing Nett, the porcupine seedling who remained on Coppergrass. Jab wanted to mention how glad he was that Yagub had his priorities in order, but he decided to save the joke for Sanu.

Meanwhile, Rattarossa's plan was to travel with his troops. The other Barkheart Order knights marched to the trade routes between Kraksnout and ZelZaytun, which would cut off trade and more supplies to the Holy City. It also meant Rattarossa would find Rattin.

The kings agreed to rendezvous at the lake depot south of ZelZaytun, the same spot Nasalid had attacked a few months ago, the same spot Jab returned to in his nightmares.

Jab's feelings were jumbled. His hometown could be razed or its citizens brought into the city to starve. Sanu had sworn King Ridgerd would want a direct and daring assault on ZelZaytun based on how the king played double siege. Jab couldn't believe how foolish they had been.

Splitting up was a mistake. Jab was in over his head and prayed that Sanu fared better.

As a fellow Qawari squirrel, Yagub should have been more sympathetic to how Jab was feeling, but the lovestruck teen was growing more forlorn with each passing day.

Marching south by southwest, Jab would traverse a part of Qawar he'd never visited before. The jagged coastline supposedly boasted lots of animals and plants he'd never seen. Sanu once said there were monkeys, but that sounded ridiculous.

The sea breeze brought a salty tang to the air as it brushed Jab's cheek. He rode a horse, sharing a saddle with Brouglas. He had to sit in front of him, which was uncomfortable, but behind him would have Jab sitting on his tail. Jab at least had the luxury of letting his tail hang over the horse, but if it came time for a battle, he'd have to dismount. Jab looked over his shoulder, measuring the thousands-strong army, and shivered, despite the brutal Qawari sun.

Then he looked ahead at the king, flanked by banner carriers, a trumpeter, and the two Barkheart knights.

"Sir Brouglas," Jab said, "do you know why those two knights are here?"

The beaver knight sighed. "Do you want the stated reason or the actual one?"

Jab relaxed a little, knowing he wasn't the only one being mysterious. "Both."

"Rattarossa said these two wished to fight alongside Ridgerd and learn from him. They wanted to be legendary warriors like him.

Ridgerd thinks it's because Rattarossa guessed how uncomfortable the king gets around seedlings and saplings who don't know him to be a good rodent. It's also possible that they are spying on him and reporting things back to Rattarossa."

Though Jab was relieved the two enemies of Qawar didn't get along better, it baffled him. "They're on the same side though. Why can't they cooperate?"

Brouglas inhaled deeply and pointed toward the coast. "Beautiful palm trees over there. Those trees, this breeze, this whole place... it's so wonderful. One might forget there's a war happening."

"Are you dodging my question?" Jab preferred Yagub's melancholy silence to whatever Brouglas was doing.

"Not at all. I'm just telling you that your home is beautiful. Haven't I always said that, Yagub?"

"I guess," Yagub mumbled.

Brouglas rolled his eyes and focused on Jab again. "The two kings aren't really on the same side, you see. Ridgerd is a war-pilgrim."

Jab wanted to point out how ridiculous that idea was, but chose to remain silent. A pilgrimage was an outward journey to find inner peace, not destroying someone's home.

"Rattarossa, though, he is a conqueror. You've heard how he gets about that emperor title."

For so long, Jab had gotten used to calling Nasalid the "Liberator," but now he wondered if he was just another conqueror and would-be emperor. With his liberation of Qawar, plus the territory he'd already conquered on the other neighboring islands, Nasalid controlled more territory than the Five Princes ever had back in Jab's grandparents' time. Jab hated the idea of Qawar just being a mere battleground for others to play politics and kingdom-expansion.

Brouglas nudged him and pointed into the distance. "What's that town up ahead?"

"Sqirlib." Jab's time looking at maps with Kash—the scout who initially recruited Jab into Nasalid's army back when Jab had believed Sanu was dead—had educated him about the town's location. Jab wondered if Kash had any family here, and if they knew he'd died saving Jab's life. Kash had been like an older brother when Jab needed one. And Jab had barely taken any time to mourn him.

King Ridgerd pulled away from the front of the marching line, slowing his stride enough so Jab and Brouglas would come up to his side. Though he was sitting atop a horse, Jab barely met the king's eye line.

"I figured I'd ask young Jab, since poor Yagub is dour about missing his sweetheart," the king said. "My scouts tell me that Sqirlib is loyal to Nasalid, that the Sprouters here were never friendly to the old Kraksnout garrison."

Jab fought the sarcasm brimming inside him. No Qawari rodent could've been sympathetic to the Frenglese, and Nasalid was a good ruler, so of course they would be loyal to him. "A friend of mine was from Sqirlib," Jab said, proud of himself for not clenching his teeth. "They were forced to give most of their fish to the garrison at Kraksnout, which made them resentful."

Ridgerd nodded. "I can't say I blame them. It amazes me how Sprouters and Grovekeepers can get along here, even with Mulchers around."

Jab didn't know how to nicely say that rodents cooperate just fine when they are nice to those who are different from them and respect each other's space, which the Frenglese invaders didn't bother trying to do. "We all lived together in harmony before the invasions started."

"Are you saying I can't talk them out of supporting Nasalid?" Ridgerd asked.

A twinge of guilt twisted Jab's heart. The king *was* trying to avoid a fight.

"Please leave them alone," Jab said. "They're no threat to you."

"Enemies!" The shout came from the front with a thick accent. Jab tore his gaze from Ridgerd, noticing raised spears in the distance, sunlight catching the spearpoints.

Ridgerd stiffened. "It seems the decision has been made for me." He raised his sword and faced the horde behind him. "Form up, lads! To war!"

13

SANU

"My grandpa still had nightmares about the Barkhearts. He was old enough to remember Zel Yorbua."

"Forget them, I'm soiling my armor thinking about Ridgerd Steelfur that Ayrim told us about. I heard his army is just there to carry his spare weapons and that he does all the fighting himself."

"You have to realize how fake that sounds."

"Could you imagine Nasalid or one of his commanders doing the same?"

"Ha! Nasalid is a good rodent, and the wisest jird in the Great Sea, but he's too old for that."

— Overheard chatter among the camp followers

In the two days since running away, Sanu realized how slow he'd been moving with the Sprouters compared with Nasalid's troops and messengers. Marching from ZelZaytun to Kraksnout had taken a full week. Sanu, Mahar, Ayrim, and the emissaries' few camp followers approached the Holy City already. A simple glance at his traveling companions explained why. The Sprouters were laden with heavy metal armor, but Nasalid had everyone dress in gear more appropriate to the weather. The lighter clothes meant lighter hindpaws and less work for the horses, so they moved faster and needed fewer breaks.

They neared the Holy City's first gatehouse, and Sanu tensed. He'd been inside before when Brouglas rescued him at the Battle of Rattin's Horns. He'd spent the following month there, living among the Frenglese Sprouters, descendants of the conquerors who'd killed his grandparents.

Cladh was in that city, that wonderful hamster who taught him Frenglese and about the Sprouter faith. ZelZaytun, where a politician taught him how to fight while stealing information from him that he would later use to hurt Grovekeepers. ZelZaytun, where Jab had mistaken Sanu for an assassin and shot a crossbow bolt at him. Thankfully, it missed, which was more than Sanu could say of the mole rat who attacked him back on Coppergrass Isle.

Ayrim snapped Sanu from his thoughts. "ZelZaytun has not changed much in the last two months, except the invaders' stink has mostly gone. Cleaning the city with rose water was a smart idea."

Sanu chuckled awkwardly. "That was actually my brother's idea."

"Ah." Ayrim clicked his tongue. "He did a good thing letting you escape. It's nice to have a sibling you can count on. My sister helped me get my job. Though, maybe she shouldn't have. It was supposed to be a straightforward siege."

Sanu hoped Jab knew how much he appreciated him.

They came so close to the city that the olive Gnaverwood blocked out the sun, and for a moment, the temperature dropped like a breeze had just gone through.

Sanu looked over his shoulder, spying Rattin's outline in the distance. So close to home, and yet he knew he may never see it again.

Mahar rode beside them. "It's a beautiful piece of architecture, isn't it? Though the work on the walls is fresh." He pointed up at the outer walls. "Those were damaged when the Liberator arrived, and he purposely made a point of not repairing them right away until the inside of the city was restored."

Sanu squinted, noticing a team of workers atop the wall. "So I guess Nasalid ordered the walls to get repaired after Rattarossa landed."

Ayrim's grip on the reins tightened. "And with Ridgerd Steelfur here, that might not be enough. The walls might need another layer."

"I don't think walls could stop that hamster," Mahar muttered. "He was so tall he could jump over."

Sanu knew that was ridiculous, since the walls were twice as tall as most buildings he'd seen, but he was fascinated at how King Ridgerd had implanted on their minds. Then he remembered how Ridgerd had shot a porcupine quill out of a trumpet like a blow dart and knew the king deserved his reputation. And Steelfur *did* sound cool.

They arrived at the double gates, which were two sections of crisscrossed steel. Mahar pointed to the falcon feathers in his headwraps, Ayrim lifted his messenger's banner, and the gates clinked open for them.

The *racka-click* of the rising gates reminded Sanu too much of a crossbow's clicking gears. Never hearing another crossbow loading again would be too soon. The camp followers departed, bidding Mahar and Ayrim farewell.

"Don't mind them," Mahar said. "They're taking our leftover supplies to the workers on the wall."

More rodents packed the city's stone streets than two months ago.

Mulchers strolled paw-in-paw, chatting. Sanu only knew what their religion was by the twigs rolled into their beards, and most Mulchers happened to be red squirrels. A group of kids crowded a sheltercake bakery, and a crowd of adults filed into a Grovekeeper prayer house.

Sanu had never seen so many species of rodent before. While Sprouters and Grovekeepers could be any species, seeing rodents wear Ganan's Rake symbols in their clothes or jewelry and the headwraps adorning some heads proved that all three All-Planter religions were represented here, cooperating in harmony.

Soft stringed instrumental music carried through the town, rising over the noise of wagon wheels and haggling over goods. Toy shops, book stores, eateries, and shops Sanu couldn't identify lined the streets. This was a liberated city.

A pit grew in Sanu's stomach, knowing this paradise would fall in seconds if Ridgerd and Rattarossa had their way.

They rounded a corner, arriving at the old military quarter of the city, which was blocked off by another gate. Sanu spied the sandy training pit where he'd learned the power of the devilbeak weapon firstpaw. They were near the city's Gananhall, where Cladh's new headquarters would be, and they were also close to the old palace used by the ancient Mulcher kings, where he assumed Nasalid would be.

But Nasalid wasn't in the palace, ruling like an emperor. The Liberator was in the military quarter, outside, speaking with soldiers.

Sanu hadn't spent much time with the imposing jird, and was jealous of the time Jab had with him. He doubted Nasalid would remember him at all.

"Hail, Liberator!" Mahar called.

The jird lifted a finger to whoever he was speaking with and turned around.

Upon spying Sanu, he smiled and waved the three of them over.

Now Sanu would witness the full extent of Nasalid's fury, because they needed to explain

76 - FAMILIES BROKEN

their failure. While Nasalid was known for his generosity, finding out three thousand prisoners were slaughtered would put that to the test.

14

JAB

As a lad, my brother and I had wild theories about why we got only nibbles of olive at the Offering Meal. We call it a "meal," and yet the food we get is less than a snack. I understand now that it is food of the soul, not the stomach. With that understanding, each morsel becomes a feast. You remain my strength, Ganan. Blest be You. Thank you.

- *From the prayer journal of Sir Brouglas*

A long row of Nasalid's mounted archers protected the coastal town of Sqirlib. The mounted archers matched Ridgerd's numbers, not to mention they had the advantage of a hilltop position. A shiver rattled down Jab's spine. If King Ridgerd lost here, Jab worried Nasalid's soldiers wouldn't recognize him. He couldn't spot Nasalid's command tent in the distance, but that might not mean anything. Nasalid, the jird who Grovekeepers called "Liberator," could be here or on the other side of the island. Jab could very well die alongside these Sprouters.

"Form ranks," King Ridgerd shouted, breaking Jab's thoughts. "We have the sun and we're out of range." The royal hamster's knights formed a thin line. Heavily armored and under a hot sun, these troops could never catch Nasalid's riders.

"Hold this line," Ridgerd commanded. "They'll come to us once they see me. Let Nasalid's war dogs make the first move."

Jab remembered the battle at Rattin's horns. Nasalid hadn't been there, and his lieutenants had used fire, pinning the Sprouter forces into a ring of death. There could be some traps here. Jab eyed the king, who measured up his soldiers.

If Jab warned him, Grovekeepers could die. If he didn't warn him, then Rattarossa could steal Ridgerd's command and kingdom, which would also mean the death of Ridgerd, Brouglas, and Yagub, three rodents who had defended both Jab and Sanu's lives.

"Brouglas," Jab whispered, "Do you remember the fire at Rattin's horns?"

"Hard to forget," Brouglas replied. He turned to the king. "My king, Yagub, Jab, and I will check the perimeter. Nasalid once boxed in a squadron of knights with fire. We'll ensure there's no oil or incendiaries."

Ridgerd glanced at them over his shoulder, waving his permission.

Yagub tsked. "Why are we going away from the action?"

Jab formed a retort, but two horses whinnying interrupted him.

In the middle of Ridgerd's formation, the two Barkheart Order knights charged forward, devilbeaks in the air.

"What?" Ridgerd roared. "Get back here, pellet heads!"

The other soldiers, both mounted knights and infantry, gaped at their commander. The king glared at the charging knights.

After a deep breath, Ridgerd raised his claymore over his head. "We're all brothers in Ganan, Blest be Him. The sun will ruin the archers' eyes. Trust in the steel. Charge!"

Brouglas yanked the reins and pulled him and Jab away from the charging rodents, who were all shouting a war-cry that rattled Jab's eardrums.

Arrows blackened the sky like a murder of crows from the Droughtlands.

"Ridgerd will get them killed," Yagub said as Ridgerd's troops closed the distance, an arrow-swarm descending on them. "That's a death march."

"Best not to look," Brouglas replied, forcing himself to block Jab's view of the charging line.

After watching Sanu fall from a high rock and get swallowed by fire, Jab wasn't about to be fooled again by a battle's insanity. He slunk off the horse, using his tail to squirm out of the saddle.

Arrows rained onto Ridgerd's forces, plinking onto their armor like hail on metal.

The charge continued with most of the soldiers unfazed. Two horses struggled on the ground, left behind by the others, and five infantry rodents lay writhing in the dirt. Hundreds of arrows littered the grass, stuck in place like reeds in a marsh. Sanu watched Ridgerd's troops run up the hill, but he had to shield his eyes. Their steel armor was too shiny to look at for long, which must have messed with the archers' aim.

Nasalid's soldiers swapped bows for spears, and Ridgerd's knights slammed into them. King Ridgerd himself was easy enough to follow because of his crown helmet. He cut down Nasalid's troops so fast that a circle of space opened around him.

"He's doing it," Brouglas muttered. "Look!" Half the camp followers had abandoned their tasks to watch alongside Jab.

The blacksmiths and carpenters dropped their tools and all exclaimed the same thing. "Steelfur!"

Nasalid's troops parted from Ridgerd, bumping into each other as they scrambled away from him. A double horn blew from behind the hill, a signal Jab had learned in Nasalid's camp.

Retreat.

Nasalid's riders pulled back and descended the hill's other side.

"There's no oil here. This was no trap." Brouglas faced the camp followers. "Come on, let's join the king." He leaned over his horse and helped Jab climb back into the saddle. "Yagub, tend to the fallen. It'll be good practice for when you're in the order."

"At once," Yagub replied.

Brouglas and Jab galloped forward, and Jab's eyes followed the retreating mounted archers. It shouldn't have been this way. Those Barkheart knights had acted so foolishly, and yet, Ridgerd changed his plan on the spot and turned this into a victory.

The archers thundered away, their ranks only a little thinner than before. Even though Jab hadn't spent much time on this side of Qawar, he knew those soldiers were falling back to ZelZaytun, where they'd have to fight another day.

Atop the hill, Ridgerd's troops cheered, though with less gusto than in their charge. With the sun beating down on Jab's neck, he got an idea why.

That same armor that saved them from the arrow downpour had exhausted them. They'd have to stop their advance, drink a lake's worth of water, and eat a farm's worth of food. And on the other side of the hill, Sqirlib town sat defenseless, abandoned by Nasalid's soldiers.

A mounted porcupine trudged down the hill, meeting Jab and Brouglas halfway. "It's good you're here," the porcupine said. "The king needs you to translate something."

Jab wondered what it could possibly be as he summited the hill.

Atop, the knights patted their horses and each other on the back while throwing their helmets into the grass and sucking air. The king stood with his sword plunged into the dirt, leaning into it like a cane. He'd removed his gauntlets, revealing sweaty paws. He gasped for air like he'd been running for hours instead of fighting for minutes.

"Brouglas!" the king called between breaths. "That ... sign..." He pulled a paw from his sword hilt and pointed at a wooden sign.

The beaver dismounted and bowed before the king. "Congratulations on your victory," Brouglas said. "But I cannot read Qawari letters."

Still on the horse, Jab stiffened. "I can."

The king nodded, wiping matted fur out of his eyes. "Tell us ... its message ... and inform ... the townsrodents ... they are in our care."

As he finished speaking, a soldier who'd been struggling to remove his armor collapsed. The sun reflected off him like a lighthouse.

Jab urged the horse forward, and descended the hill toward the town and the sign. Streaks of paint dripped from the letters, and drops in the dirt around the sign suggested it was fresh. The town's houses reminded Jab of Rattin, but none showed signs of activity. Jab squinted at the sign.

Hello, Frengs. We invite you to visit Sqirlib as unarmed pilgrims another time. We knew you were coming, and emptied the town of food and supplies. There are dead animals in the cisterns. Turn around.

Jab's heart raced. This had been a trap. The cisterns held all the town's spare water. If they'd put dead animals in there, not a drop would be safe to drink now. If Ridgerd won more battles like this, he would surely lose the war. But if Nasalid had to abandon towns and poison water to do it, Jab wasn't sure if it was a war worth winning.

15

SANU

The General made me research wars among the Frenglese and Rottelanders to see how they fight. Reading various accounts, I can say with certainty that I question how much Sprouters understand what it means to believe in Ganan if they call him "the peace king." I wonder if they'll return to fighting each other after they finish their business in Qawar.

- Diaries of General Ironseed's secretary

In the Holy City of ZelZaytun, Sanu stood before Nasalid, the jird who Grovekeepers all across the Great Sea called "Liberator." Though this was their second time meeting, Sanu felt like they were both different rodents now. Nasalid's tawny fur carried new flecks of gray, and dark circles under his eyes suggested a reduced sleeping schedule. And with Sanu's damaged ear from his misadventure on Coppergrass, he certainly looked different too.

"Serenity to your family." Sanu inclined his head. "It's good to see you again, Liberator."

"Tranquility to your home. And it is good to see *you*, Savior of Rattin. I would like to hear about what happened to your ear and how your brother is doing, but I understand you have more pressing news to share." Nasalid shifted his gaze from Sanu to Mahar and Ayrim.

Ayrim stared at his hindpaws. "The negotiations failed."

"That's one way to put it," Mahar scoffed. "Emperor Rattarossa ordered the prisoners taken at the failed siege..." He shot a glance at Ayrim, then took a deep breath. "To be executed. He threw them over the walls of Kraksnout. There must have been thousands."

"Three thousand," Ayrim said. "We were speaking with Ridgerd, one of the Frenglese kings."

Nasalid covered his mouth with his paw, shaking his head. "He slaughtered prisoners?"

Sanu stepped forward. "King Ridgerd didn't know about it. It was Rattarossa's way to undercut negotiations."

"Inconceivable." Nasalid's nostrils flared. "This treachery is unheard of. Prisoners or no, they were still rodents with families. This city is full of Sprouter trinkets. I would've given all of them and then some for those prisoners."

"There are some Barkheart Order knights held prisoner outside the city," Ayrim said. "Pay the Sprouters back by killing them."

Nasalid and Ayrim were about the same height, but somehow, the grizzled jird managed to loom over him, and he placed a paw on the hilt of his scimitar. "All rodents have dignity. I will kill an enemy soldier but will not slaughter the unarmed and harmless. Killing prisoners is monstrous. I recommend you take the time to re-read the Divine Poetics."

Reading the holy books had always been more of Jab's passion, but Sanu did know a few parts, one of which was the rules about warfare. The All-Planter threatened wicked generals with an eternity in the Droughtlands. Watching Nasalid grip his sword reminded Sanu of Ridgerd, another powerful rodent who was terrified of being sent to the Droughtlands.

Maybe those two really could find common ground.

Ayrim hunched. "Understood, sir. I'll head to the prayer hall now." Ayrim shoved his paws into his pockets and departed.

"What is our response, Liberator?" Mahar asked. "My brother Zaqar is in Rattin. I can send him a message quickly."

"We have nothing to say to the invaders." Nasalid turned to one of the nobles he'd been speaking to before. "Send a rider to the regiment that rode to defend Sqirlib. Inform them I will reinforce their numbers so they can attempt another siege against Kraksnout." He turned to the other. "Have the warships patrol the east and north coasts. Commandeer any fishing vessels used by the enemy. We'll block

Kraksnout from the sea. The invaders will have no reinforcements."

Sanu's heart and stomach switched places. If Ridgerd was out marching, he and his troops would starve. And while his and Jab's plan was for him to stick with King Ridgerd, it could have failed and Jab could be with that Rattarossa monster instead. He just hoped Jab was safe, away from the fighting.

A sharp nudge from Mahar made Sanu look up. Nasalid stood over him.

"You're troubled," the Liberator said. "Speak."

Despite his drying mouth, Sanu responded. "I spent the last month mostly with King Ridgerd. I know what kind of a rodent he is. He believes that he's going to be sent to the Droughtlands and his only way out is to retake ZelZaytun. When you sent me and Jab to Freng, Ridgerd's father had just died. His father's last words to him were to reinforce Lady Marjitay's forces here, since he didn't know she'd failed against you. I had got it in my head that he was a good rodent, but knowing how smart he is, I'm not so sure he didn't know Rattarossa would kill the prisoners. I'm worried he just wants to fight for the sake of fighting."

"I see." Nasalid stroked his beard. "I had become worried when you never reported back. In all honesty, part of my fury at the invaders has been guided by thinking they killed you and Jab."

"No, Sir Brouglas protected us."

"I thought that Sprouter was a good beaver. And my sergeant who accompanied you? Jandi?"

Sanu blew a slow exhale. "He drowned. When Ridgerd decided to invade, he put us on one of his boats. Jab and Jandi both fell overboard, and Sir Brouglas dove into the ocean to save Jab. Nobody ever found Jandi, but he was wearing a full set of armor."

Nasalid leaned closer. "Your brother is alive, isn't he?"

"Yes," Sanu said hurriedly. "But Jandi couldn't have survived. I think Brouglas said he saw him sink because of his armor. Anyway, we all spent time on Coppergrass Island. Ridgerd went there to save Jab and Brouglas. He is a good hamster." The words felt both honest and wrong, especially under Mahar's glare. "At least, I thought he was. I'm really confused."

"You heard the stories," Mahar said. "How he cut down Grovekeepers like we were paper. He'll keep on killing. They call him 'Steelfur,' because they think he can't be defeated."

Sanu's damaged ear throbbed, even though it had healed. "He-he saved my life. More than once. He's not a monster," Sanu pleaded. "Wouldn't *you* do anything to keep yourself out of the Droughtlands?"

Nasalid stood straighter and gestured to the building behind them, the palace of the ancient Mulcher kings, which had been used by all three faiths. "I, too, fear the Droughtlands' heat. It's why I insisted on a council of three to rule the city instead of me. I do not wish to sit on Suleimouse's throne and I want to be done fighting."

Nasalid narrowed his eyes. "When Qawar is safe from invaders, I will return to Damouscus.

I will spend my remaining days training a successor, and the moment my successor is ready, I will step down, and return to ZelZaytun once more, but as a pilgrim." Nasalid sighed. "Seeing you has reminded me that I need to check on my own brother. He's been helping me communicate with the council as I go back and forth between the camps."

A light flickered in Sanu's heart. "Are the rodents on the council the same ones you appointed?"

Mahar groaned. "Three months ago? Yes. The former prayer warden of Rattin, the Mulcher elder from ZelAmran, plus that hamster seedling to represent the Sprouters."

"Seedling?" Sanu asked, whiskers drooping.

"Sapling," Mahar corrected. "She was one and became the other. It's hard to want to learn all the Sprouters' terms when they are killing our countryrodents."

Sanu didn't respond to the joke. He knew better than most Grovekeepers that not all Sprouters were bad. And the possibility of seeing the Sapling of ZelZaytun brightened Sanu's spirits. Not because he thought about her all the time. That would be ridiculous.

16

JAB

And in reply, Ganan said, "You tell me the pursuit of knowledge is wasted time and money. I say Blest be They who never end their quest for knowledge and understanding. Go as far as Kinoumi or the most distant island in Freng for knowledge, and then go even farther."

- Excerpt from the Ganandeeds, "Debate with the Skeptic."

Jab read the warning sign outside the abandoned town of Sqirlib to Ridgerd and his soldiers. The claim that the town was emptied and the cistern had ruined water in it was not received well.

One of the soldiers pointed a spear at Jab. "You brought a dirty Grovekeeper with us, my king. He's lying. It's their way."

Sir Brouglas stepped forward, pushing the spearpoint away. "Watch your tongue. The boy is honest."

Jab remembered his lie to the beaver and his heart sank. He'd lied so many times, but he'd always told himself it was in the interest of protecting someone or saving lives. Maybe liars deceived *themselves* most.

"Break it up," King Ridgerd said, still breathing heavily. "We're all tired."

Sir Brouglas turned toward the royal hamster. "My liege, Nasalid has been known to use poison just as much as fire. He is an honorable rodent. I would heed the warning."

Yagub plodded up from behind, out of breath. "I can vouch for him too. He read the sign correctly."

"Have you been here before, Yagub?" Jab wondered if Yagub and Kash knew each other before they joined different sides of the conflict.

"No, but my uncles visited to fish often." Yagub pointed at the docks on the other side of town. "All the ships vanished."

"At least we won the battle," the king replied. "A game of double siege continues until one general remains, and here I am, unopposed. Though seeing how many of these good rodents are close to heat exhaustion, I would've preferred a game over this."

Jab peered at the exhausted soldiers. They breathed so rapidly that they sounded like a drum line. Half of them lay on the ground, struggling to remove their armor. None of them looked like they could march another step. Even the horses seemed exhausted. It was all the heavy metal armor everyone insisted on wearing. It had saved most of them from the arrow fire, but it seemed like the sun would finish the job.

Brouglas noticed too. "My king, we can't press forward. We have to make camp and use our own provisions. We can't trust anything here."

"I walked into a trap." The king slumped and shook his head. "You, Yagub, and Jab search the town while the troops recover and the camp followers attend to them. See if anything is left that we can use." The king raised his sword in the air, and all the soldiers' eyes that could stay open fixed on him. "Fellow pilgrims, to celebrate our victory here, we shall rest for the remainder of the day and set out at first light. We suspect treachery, so we will use our own supplies instead of feeding off what's in town. If the town is deemed clear, we will rest in the homes. For now, find some shade and drink your water slowly."

Hesitant nods and grumbles responded. One soldier's armor bent in his attempt to rip it off.

Jab wasn't thrilled about searching an empty fishing village the size of his hometown, but it was better than sitting around with angry and exhausted soldiers shoving weapons in his face. The descent into Sqirlib with Brouglas and Yagub was plodding. As much as the sun beat down on Jab, he worried about how his armored friend was faring.

"Do you need more water?" Jab asked.

Brouglas shook his head. "We'll have an Offering Meal service at nightfall. I'll have a sliver of olive when we pray. That will be my sustenance today."

Jab still recoiled at the Sprouter practice of eating olives, but he'd seen how it gave the really devoted ones a kind of confidence and hope, though Jab couldn't imagine how nutritious one bite of anything could be, especially without water.

Yagub chuckled. "I hope I can match your devotion one day."

"You already do," Brouglas replied, stepping around a loose rock at the bottom of the hill. "Nobody who wants to join the Barkheart Order has a weak faith."

Jab fought the urge to scoff. Two of those Barkheart guys almost got everyone killed in the battle by defying Ridgerd's orders. The idea of Yagub in one of their suits of armor was both laughable and horrifying.

How could anyone want that?

They stepped onto the town's main path, and Jab felt like he was in a transplanted Rattin. Rows of shops hugged either side of the road, and homes stood behind them. Instead of relying on a trade road's intersection, this town had fishing docks. It was nothing compared to what he'd seen in Freng, where warships were constructed, but the little harbor could've housed a few smaller boats.

In the town's center stood two buildings of near equal height, a Gananshed and a prayer hall, the holy buildings of the Sprouters and the Grovekeepers. They might've been indistinguishable if it hadn't been for the Gananshed's sculpture of Ganan's Rake and the prayer hall's calligraphic inscription of the first line of the Divine Poetics.

"Maybe some Sprouters stayed behind in the Gananshed," Yagub suggested. "They all have basements meant to shelter orphans and the unhoused."

"I don't think so," Jab said, stepping reverently toward the first empty shop. "Nasalid would've offered them protection from the invaders."

"Invaders?" Yagub growled. "I'm *Qawari*. This island is my home."

Jab wheeled around, wondering how Sanu could've ever called this guy a friend. "And that means Ridgerd isn't your king and Rattarossa isn't your emperor, but you sure haven't been acting like it. The Sprouters who lived here were just as scared of Ridgerd and Rattarossa as the Grovekeepers would've been."

"You can't know that!"

Brouglas stepped between them. "That's enough, lads. I'm not your king either, but you'll listen to me. Jab, check the shops and houses on the left. Yagub, on the right. I'll look in the harbor. Yell if you find anything or anyone."

Jab's brow furrowed. "Fine."

"Yes, sir," Yagub replied, heading for a bakery.

Jab explored a smithy first. It was bare, with dust outlines suggesting where tools once hung. The forge had cooled, and the cabinets were empty. Not even scrap metal littered the floor.

The clothing store next door wasn't much different. A master tailor could've taken all the threads and fabric inside and struggled to make a handkerchief.

Jab tried the house behind the smithy, and all the furniture was gone. He entered the second house to similar results, and he couldn't decide whether this was a relief or annoying. He didn't want to starve, but if it meant the invaders couldn't press forward, it was a bit of a victory in its own way.

The third house gave Jab pause. A little inscription sat in the entryway. *Home of Kashdood of Sqirlib.* Jab's eyes watered. His scouting mentor, the guy who saved him from burning to death at the Battle of Rattin, was from Sqirlib. And Kash had mentioned that he was named after his father. This was the childhood home of the squirrel who had been like a big brother when he needed it most, when he'd believed Sanu was dead. Kash died in the siege of ZelZaytun, and it had been Jab's fault.

And the home was barren, save for a crumpled thobe on the floor—clothing Kash could've worn.

Knowing Kash's family was still alive and under Nasalid's protection gave him some solace, but couldn't fill the hole in his heart left by his dead friend.

17

SANU

This most holy site was visited by our Lord, Ganan the Gardener, Blest be Him. We will stop at nothing to keep this holy ground in the paws of Sprouters to honor Him. We defend this tree, the land around it, and thus we cloak our hearts in bark.

- Inscription on a copper plaque outside the palace

Approaching the ancient Palace of Mulcher Kings filled Sanu with dread and awe. Last time he went in there with Nasalid, it was at the end of the siege and Lady Marjitay murdered the Sapling, creating the job opening that Cladh filled. He read a plaque outside the building which he hadn't noticed previously in his time with the Sprouters.

Nasalid placed a paw on Sanu's shoulder. "Cladh spoke highly of you. She said your ability to learn Frenglese was astonishing and she made sure I remembered that ZelZaytun would've remained in Marjitay's clutches were it not for you and your brother's heroics."

"Thank you," Sanu said. He'd be lying if he'd said that he hadn't been thinking about Cladh constantly. She was so smart and tough. She carried her authority well and everyone respected her, even though she was a teenager. Entering the palace, he couldn't pay attention to all the religious artwork they passed under—he was too focused on seeing Cladh again and getting his paws to stop shaking.

Armored boots clanged on the floor ahead of them. A pair of squirrels appeared, carrying feathered spears and wearing plate armor with the most garish yellow frills Sanu had ever seen. Behind them strode a hamster, clad in the bright brown robes of a Sapling, with a gold-dipped acorn amulet around her neck.

Cladh.

Sanu's heart raced as she smiled at him.

She patted the guards on the biceps and they parted, allowing her to meet Sanu and Nasalid halfway. "It's good to see you again!" Her voice reverberated in the decorated halls like the hum of a plucked lute string. She wrapped Sanu in a hug. "With you gone, I feel like I've been missing my little brother." She broke from the embrace and pointed at Nasalid. "I've been telling this guy I'd stage a coup if anything happened to my buddy."

Little brother. Buddy.

Those words didn't feel like a hammer hitting his heart. Not at all. Sanu wasn't disappointed. He examined his hindpaws and Nasalid chuckled.

"Yes, and I told her I didn't appreciate jokes about Frenglese Sprouters turning against me," Nasalid said.

Cladh nudged Sanu. "He knows I kid. You *are* late though. I'm guessing you got tied up on your journey?"

Sanu scratched the back of his head. "I guess 'tied up' is one way to put it. How do you like being a Sapling?"

"Nobody orders me around anymore, though I'm sure the Arborist will have something to say to me once the war's over." Cladh folded her arms over her chest. "This Rattarossa guy is bad news. And Prince Ridgerd showing up doesn't bode well either."

"King," Nasalid corrected.

"Well, that's worse for us," Cladh replied. "He can't set hindpaw in here, you know that, right?"

"Wait," Sanu said, "another Sapling told him that if he re-took ZelZaytun, all of his sins would be forgiven. Couldn't you just tell him that's not true?"

Nasalid's small ears twitched like a second pair of eyebrows. "It can't be that easy."

Cladh shrugged. "Trying can't hurt. And maybe I could tell Rattarossa that none of his sins will be forgiven unless he turns around."

Sanu stared at his hindpaws and turned away from them. "I don't think that's a priority for him. I got to know Ridgerd and he is noble, even though he is willing to kill in a fight. But

Rattarossa is not like that at all. He wants to conquer the island."

"Defeating me would cement any man's legacy." Nasalid tapped the tip of his tail against the mosaic tile floor as if the rhythm helped him concentrate. "Any rodent who wants to be called 'emperor' is obsessed with legacy and honor. My spies tell me Rattarossa is in league with the Barkheart Order knights. Is this true?"

Cladh's voice hardened. "Your brother asked me the same thing in the last council meeting he called. Him calling our council was not part of our original agreement with you, I might add."

A stern glare passed between the hamster and the jird, and Cladh's bodyguards stiffened behind her.

"War forces us into less than desirable positions," Nasalid said icily. "The Barkheart attacks that started after we liberated the city gave me little choice."

Sanu stepped between them. "A bunch of Barkheart guys were with Rattarossa in Kraksnout."

Cladh backed off. "The Barkheart Order is mostly Rottelanders, with only a few members from Freng or Llygoden. They like the idea of a single empire uniting all Sprouters, which does match with Rattarossa's political ambitions."

"Those guys were creepy," Sanu said.

Nasalid tsked. "They committed massacres against Grovekeepers in the Invasion War, not to mention the three thousand recently added to their number of killed rodents."

"They also built houses of healing," Cladh said. "Look, I'll prepare two messages. One will go to King Ridgerd, and the other to King Rattarossa. I'll remind them of your generous offer to let any unarmed Sprouters come to ZelZaytun as pilgrims, I will vouch for the fact that Sprouters live in Qawar without any issues, and that this war is not part of the All-Planter's plan."

"I could take the message to King Ridgerd," Sanu offered. As the words left his mouth, he felt like an idiot for saying them. Jab was taking care of Ridgerd. Sanu needed to trust him. "Or I can go to Rattarossa."

"Absolutely not," Nasalid said. "You know how Ridgerd thinks. You will remain by my side and predict how he will react and respond. I need contingency plans."

Cladh's whiskers stiffened. "Nasalid is right, Sanu. It's dangerous out there."

Sanu wondered how he could explain he could handle the danger while sounding cool and also honest.

After a deep breath, Nasalid motioned toward the door. "I need those messages within the hour."

"Fine," Cladh hissed, "but only because I *also* think that the messages need to go out fast. Not because you told me to. You promised you'd let the Council of Three run the city, and you already forced your brother to babysit us. I won't let you order me around." She exhaled and wrapped Sanu in another hug. "Come see me later," she whispered. "I have an idea. There's an olive oil press behind the Gananhall. Meet me there at sunset."

Sanu smiled. Her hugs didn't take the sting out of the "little brother" and "buddy" comments, but he was glad to be close to her again. Being a buddy with her was better than nothing, and some part of him knew he was too young to ask for anything else.

18

JAB

In Phranktonbourg's ashes, I knelt in the debris where a single flower defied the soot and rubble. I will remember its vibrant purple until my last day. Beautiful nature resisting rodents' destruction. I never understood the name of "All-Planter" until that moment, and I had never been clearer on why the All-Planter sent us a Gardener. I hope the All-Planter can plant the seed of renewal in my brother's heart. And perhaps, my own.

- From the prayer journal
  of Sir Brouglas

Jab trudged back up the hill, finally out of the afternoon scorch, empty-pawed and guilt-free over finding nothing. He didn't want to help these soldiers kill Grovekeepers. He didn't wish for these soldiers to die, but he wasn't about to joyfully aid their fight. There had to be some way to send them home without any more bloodshed. He'd find it.

Since Sqirlib was abandoned and emptied as he'd warned, Jab saluted the lookout. The lookout, a beaver, peered down at him. Jab shook his head and shrugged, and the lookout waved him up.

"Nothing?" the beaver asked.

"Not a crumb, a scrap, or a thread," Jab said.

"Pellets. That's what the other squirrel said too."

The petty part of Jab was mad that Yagub had returned before him, but it wasn't a race. "Even though you see Nasalid as an enemy, he *is* honest. That sign told it true."

"Watch it, kid," the lookout replied. "The king and Sir Brouglas like you, but that doesn't mean you can talk to us like that."

Jab had been perfectly polite and was finally telling the truth, but he didn't want to upset someone holding a weapon. "I'm sorry," he said as sincerely as he could.

"Sorry for what?" a booming voice interrupted.

King Ridgerd's long shadow crept over the lookout and Jab. The crown at the top of the shadow spread out like antlers.

"Sqirlib is empty," Jab said.

"At least I won my double siege game," Ridgerd muttered. "Nice to know Nasalid is honest. I almost wish we had more rodents like him in the Freng Islands, am I right?" Ridgerd playfully shoved the lookout on the shoulder, which made the lookout's knees buckle.

Nursing his shoulder, the beaver chuckled. "An excellent observation, my king."

Jab rolled his eyes and told himself to tell Sanu about this later.

The king squinted at Sqirlib. "Nasalid thought we'd kill everyone in this town. I wouldn't have let anyone harm a single hair on the townsrodents once the soldiers surrendered." He sighed and the shift in his upper body made his metal armor whine. "That's what they think of us because of what our ancestors did in the Holy War."

"You call it the Holy War?" Jab asked. That name was almost as insulting as when they'd renamed ZelZaytun to erase the Grovekeeper identity, masking the slaughter of the inhabitants.

Ridgerd's tone softened. "I suppose a Qawari Grovekeeper wouldn't find it very holy." He crouched to meet Jab's eyes. "I know what my grandfather did. He, Lady Marjitay's grandfather, and a regiment of Barkheart Order knights. I know about the exile and massacre. I am not them. I do not wish to repeat history. Please believe me."

Jab's tail stiffened, along with his spine. "You *are* repeating history just by being here."

"Hey!" the lookout said, gripping his spear tighter. "You can't talk to the king like that."

Ridgerd shot him an icy glare. "I wish more people did. I prefer direct and honest speech to people agreeing with everything I say." He turned back to Jab, tone cooling. "The All-Planter sent me on this mission because I am not like that generation. I want our faiths to live side by side in harmony."

"They already were." Jab had seen it for himself. Nasalid set up a Mulcher, Sprouter, and Grovekeeper to rule ZelZaytun together. Prayer halls were restored.

A cold silence hung between them.

Footsteps behind them broke the awkward moment as Sir Brouglas stomped up the hill. "No ships in the harbor, I couldn't even find a fishing hook." He glanced at the king and Jab and arched an eyebrow. "What's wrong?"

Facing Brouglas, Jab pointed at Ridgerd. "He doesn't see himself for what he truly is." Jab's heart pumped faster than it had in recent memory and he got in Ridgerd's face. "Is there still blood on your sword? It could belong to some of my family members. Distant cousins, of course. I'm sure Sanu told you we're orphans. My parents couldn't afford medicine since Lady Marjitay controlled the trade routes. That wouldn't have happened if there weren't a Freng monarch ruling where she had no business being."

A line of moisture beaded in the king's eyes, and he stood to his full height. Tears trickled down his fur, but he didn't bother to wipe them. "I'm truly sorry about your parents, Sanu. You don't know the burden of rule. You don't know what it's like having religious leaders tell you that you're destined for the Droughtlands. You don't understand how Nasalid's offer of pilgrimage sounded like a threat."

Jab held up a finger to correct the king after mistaking him for his brother, but Ridgerd gulped, startling him.

Two thin lines matted the fur under the king's eyes. He gestured to the camp behind him and the hundreds of soldiers. "The troops that I brought with me, I can't say their hearts are all pure, but they honestly believe this campaign is their way into the Walled Garden. You have my word that none of them will harm any innocents. If even one does, I will deal with him harshly. Perhaps if we can reach Olihort before Rattarossa, I can treat with Nasalid. We can avoid total bloodshed. That is my heart's wish. But you must understand that if I turn around now, without even trying, losing my kingdom will be the least of my concerns. My father's strength is the one thing keeping the other Frenglese kings in check. They'll fight each other, and then Rattarossa will plow over the remnants. More death."

Jab curled his tail. There was already more death, and he hadn't stopped Rattarossa's mass murder. "If you want to get to the lake before your rival, then you had better get a move on." Jab doubted that Rattarossa would've given even a moment for a conversation like this. Jab somehow hated and respected the hamster in front of him.

A tiny smile parted the king's snout. "I was enjoying our verbal game of double siege. Perhaps you'll allow me a game one night. Your brother is quite skilled."

Nothing about this made Jab want to play games, but a rumble in the distance made him pause.

Hooves thundered, enough for a battalion of troops.

King Ridgerd punched the lookout in the same shoulder as before, but without the playfulness. "Some watch you are!"

A winded Yagub ran over from camp. "My king, it's the same riders we engaged earlier!"

Ridgerd's paw flew to his sword, unsheathing it faster than Jab could breathe. "They've come to test our mettle once more?" He stomped toward the direction of the sound.

The riders weren't coming toward them, but going at an angle, retracing the path that Ridgerd's force had marched that morning.

"Back to Kraksnout," Brouglas said. "That wasn't a real retreat then. They are going to harass Kraksnout now that we've departed."

Jab's eyes widened. The king's soldiers were too tired to chase them, and pursuit would mean losing their progress.

Ridgerd sheathed his sword, and headed toward the stirring soldiers. "Listen up, lads! They are inviting us to chase them back to Kraksnout. I didn't see any battering rams or catapults, did you? Our comrades at Kraksnout are quite safe from horse archers. We need to continue our march south. Let's not fall for their tricks."

Jab stepped beside Brouglas where he could get a better view of the congregated soldiers. They still looked bedraggled, way thinner than their armor made them seem.

Yagub jogged to get beside the king. "Let's go, men! To Olihort!"

Jab winced. Yagub really was a traitor.

"This is getting out of paw," Brouglas said. "I think we need to get that meeting between the king and Nasalid. Do you believe Ridgerd, Jab? That he wants to end this with as little harm as possible?"

Sanu trusted him, and Jab was the one who had problems telling the truth.

Jab sighed, unwilling to lie to his protector. "No."

19

SANU

"There's no way he killed twenty soldiers by himself in one battle."

"That's why they call him Ridgerd Steelfur."

"He's why they retreated."

"I heard they were supposed to retreat. It was Nasalid's trick."

"Call it what you want, but our boys broke ranks because of him."

— Overheard chatter in ZelZaytun

Sanu hurried out of the prayer hall once he finished his prayers. Sunset cast ZelZaytun in an orange shadowy glow. Nasalid was swamped by advisers and important rodents in the city, so Sanu's escape went unnoticed. He navigated through the streets, alone in the fading light. Torches and lanterns glowed in shops. The physical space of the city hadn't changed much since Sanu's time here when Lady Marjitay ruled, but he noticed a difference.

Even though he heard panicked whispers about the two Sprouter kings, there seemed to be a greater ease between Mulcher, Sprouter, and Grovekeeper. Pilgrims from one faith got directions from citizens of another religion. This seemed like the dream everyone had wanted, and Ridgerd's presence here threatened that dream and felt like a rock in Sanu's gut.

The Gananhall near the grove around the Gnaverwood tree was one of the few buildings visible from blocks away, and its shadow profile of Ganan's Rake made it impossible to miss from this side of the Gnaverwood. Sprouters filtered into the Gananhall, which boasted a tower allowing for a higher view of the olive tree's trunk. He wondered how many of them knew that their Grovekeeper neighbors refused to look at the tree while it was in Lady Marjitay's paws.

Skirting around the long worship hall took almost as long as it did to walk there. He rounded a corner into an alley behind the Gananhall, where he found Cladh, standing beside a burly squirrel. She wasn't in her ornate brown Sapling robes, and her bodyguard from before was dressed like any commoner off the street. Cladh leaned against a circular stone table, which had a big stone wheel on it, attached to a wooden lever. Approaching it, he caught a salty whiff.

An olive press. Since Grovekeepers abstained from the tree's fruit, he'd never seen one, and he would've guessed it was a grain press if he didn't know better. The distinct aroma reminded him of his time on Coppergrass Isle.

"Good job finding us," Cladh said.

"Thanks, I almost didn't recognize you." Sanu had no clue why those words left his mouth. He'd thought about her face every day and she still looked beautiful in regular clothing, maybe even more so. He'd recognized her before realizing she was dressed differently. Those ceremonial robes she had to wear looked so gaudy, almost as ostentatious as using the word ostentatious.

Cladh pushed off the olive press and approached Sanu. "My messages for the two kings went to Nasalid, but I have an itchy feeling that he's not going to send them."

"Why?"

"I think he wants to kill them." Cladh let the words wash over Sanu before continuing. "Rodents have always grumbled about Nasalid's generosity. Some criticize him and say his generosity to the Frenglese that he fought was a sign of weakness. And with rumors about Ridgerd's battle prowess being so rampant and Rattarossa's ambitions so obvious, I think Nasalid wants to make sure he remains the main power in this part of the Great Sea. The massacre of all those prisoners is not helping things either."

Sanu curled his tail tight. With so much riding on the charisma and personalities of Ridgerd and Rattarossa, killing them both might be enough to end the expedition, forcing their soldiers to retreat from Qawar. While he didn't like the idea of Ridgerd being killed, Sanu wasn't as convinced of his invincibility as everyone else.

"If Nasalid kills them, do you think the Frengs and Rottelanders will go home?" Sanu asked.

Cladh arched an eyebrow. "I'm worried they'll fight harder or come back with even more troops, which is why I wanted to meet with you. You have to make absolutely sure Ridgerd gets this message. I made a third copy."

Her bodyguard coughed.

Cladh rolled her eyes. "Whima's writing skills are so beautiful that I asked him to make a third copy for me." She stuck out her tongue at the squirrel, then winked at Sanu. I need someone I can trust and who knows the land and knows Ridgerd. You're the only rodent who is all those things. Whima agreed to ride out with you."

Sanu's heart raced. He and Jab had agreed that Jab would be the one to stay with Ridgerd and Sanu would find Nasalid. Nasalid had demanded that Sanu remain with him. If he did what Nasalid asked, Ridgerd might wind up dead, triggering another war. If Sanu snuck away with Cladh's message, he'd be betraying Nasalid and Jab's trust.

But maybe Jab would want him to improvise and adapt to this new information. Everything hinged on getting the two kings to retreat on their own. That was the only way to stop the killing.

Sanu took a deep breath. "Nasalid might already be looking for me. Can we leave now?"

Cladh wiggled her whiskers. "I was hoping you'd say that." She motioned for Sanu to follow her, and she advanced along the back edge of the Gananhall's outer wall, which led to a horse stall. "After Lady Marjitay murdered the last Sapling, I thought it would be a good idea to keep a spare horse back here in case any other messed up politicians tried to copy her actions. Thankfully, Sir Brouglas's old horse needed a home."

Sanu peered around the stall's edge, finding the familiar face and mane of Vermitch. Sanu gave him a gentle pat on the neck. "Hey buddy," Sanu said. "Remember me?"

Cladh reached into her pocket and pulled out a carrot. "He's finicky. Give him a snack and he'll love you forever."

Sanu accepted it and fed the horse, who munched happily.

"Anything to pack?" Whima asked.

Sanu couldn't explain why, but he was surprised to hear the older squirrel speak. "Um, no. I've been empty-pawed for a while."

Whima pointed at the scimitar on Sanu's belt. "Not quite true."

Sanu had momentarily forgotten about his weapon, Dad's last possession. He'd always imagined using this against some faceless Sprouter invader, fighting for glory in Nasalid the Liberator's horde. And now he wanted nothing more than to save one Sprouter's life.

Whima helped Sanu onto Vermitch, and they bade farewell to Cladh. Sanu wondered if he'd see her or Nasalid again.

20

JAB

In holy Qawar, the ancient Mulchers often believed earthquakes to be signs of the All-Planter's anger. When Ganan entered the village of Taililee, tremors rumbled through the land, and the elders blamed Ganan. A crack opened in the ground, and Ganan placed his rake over it. The earthquake ended, and flowers sprouted from the crack. The elders repented and Ganan welcomed them. A garden remains there today.

- Excerpt from the Ganandeeds, "Taililee's Earthquake."

Jab hitched his pack to Sir Brouglas's horse and climbed on, ready to leave the abandoned town of Sqirlib. Even though Ridgerd had won the battle, Nasalid's troops now had a better position and Ridgerd had lost a few soldiers to heat exhaustion and a pawful were too weakened from dehydration to be much use in another battle. Jab took no joy watching Ridgerd's rodents suffer, but it was hard to find pity for invaders. He certainly preferred Ridgerd to Rattarossa though.

Sir Brouglas climbed onto the horse and Yagub jogged up beside them.

"I warned the king that we're nearing the marshlands," Yagub said. "There should be a good thicket of cedars ahead."

Brouglas nodded. "We should be ready for an ambush. It's easy to hide in trees, especially for squirrels."

Jab and Yagub shared a glance, mutually unsure if they should be bothered by his comment.

The king plodded forward, leading his horse by the reins while a panting soldier sat atop it. Jab couldn't believe the sight. Sanu had told Jab about Ridgerd's character but seeing it was another matter. The king preferred walking to horseback if one of his companions was injured. It didn't seem kingly, but neither did charging in the front lines.

"This road will lead to the lake south of the Holy City?" Ridgerd asked.

"Yes," Yagub said. "We will need a day at full speed."

Ridgerd turned to the readying troops behind him. "Three days, lads! Don't push yourself too hard. We'll come to a lake and we can all drink our fill. Be wary of hidden attackers in the forest."

Jab squinted at the horizon. They must be farther from the forest than he realized. He knew from his studies in the prayer hall that the west half of the island received more rainfall than the east half. It had something to do with the Gnaverwood and the position of the sun during the seasons. All Jab really understood from that was he loved rain and saw it as a blessing since he had grown up near a desert.

The host marched forward on Ridgerd's command, and Brouglas didn't say much as they traveled. After at least an hour of trekking, not a single tree had come in sight, save the mighty Gnaverwood. Jab's anxiety spiked. He knew they were moving slower than he was used to, but something had to be wrong. He glanced up to get an idea of the sun's position. They were definitely heading south since the Gnaverwood was getting bigger, but they should've seen the forest by now. Every map of Qawar he'd ever seen had a forest south of Sqirlib.

Something was wrong.

Yagub had noticed too.

"Sir Brouglas, we're moving too slowly," Yagub said.

"The king doesn't want anyone to exhaust themselves," the beaver replied. "Just think about how nice that forest shade will feel."

Jab scratched the back of his head. "We should've seen it by now. We're going in the right direction."

From the front, Ridgerd called out, "Lads, a stream! We'll drink up and collect our strength."

Cheers followed, and Jab wondered if they knew they should boil the water first. If Nasalid's troops had sabotaged a cistern with dead animals, they could have done something similar here.

The hundreds of soldiers behind him picked up their pace and came to the stream the king promised. While they all drank, Jab examined the horizon again from the vantage of horseback. He didn't see any trees, but he saw plenty of stumps, and a vague outline of a canopy in the distance.

Brouglas dismounted. "What's wrong? Not thirsty?"

Jab pointed into the distance. "I might know why we haven't seen the forest yet."

Yagub gasped. "Loggers have been through here. And not good ones."

"What do you mean?" Jab asked.

Sir Brouglas approached the stream. "Good loggers only take some of the trees and plant new ones when they're done. This patch might not grow back."

Curious, Jab dismounted and watched the other soldiers in the stream; they each had two flasks to fill. They all filled the first with water from the stream, and then poured water from another flask into it, closed the seal, and swirled it around before drinking.

"Brouglas, what are they doing?" Jab asked.

"Pouring vinegar into their water," Brouglas replied. "Not for flavor, of course. It purifies the water. I told the king about Nasalid's former adviser's trick with poison and we're all a bit cautious, as I'm sure you can understand. Not to mention their trick at Sqirlib."

Jab's mouth puckered at the thought, but he needed water and knew Sir Brouglas was a survivor. As Jab crouched down to cup some water, a rushed *clop-clop-clop* of hooves raced toward them. The line of soldiers parted, allowing room for a rider to approach, wearing the simple maroon garb Jab recognized as denoting a Sprouter seedling. The hooded mole rat carried a messenger's flag. "A message for the king!" The accent reminded Jab of what he'd heard on Coppergrass Isle.

The royal hamster left the stream to face the messenger. "Hello. You must be tired from your journey. Would you like some food or drink before your message?"

The mole rat removed his hood, and a childish part of Jab wondered if he'd see any of the mole rats he'd met on Coppergrass again, but he didn't recognize this person. "No, my king. This is urgent. Kraksnout is under siege once again. I avoided them, but troops from Nasalid are approaching the castle as we speak."

"We know," the king sighed. "I decided to trust the garrison to fend them off."

"I see," the mole rat said. "The original message I was to send to you comes from Freng."

"Which island?" Ridgerd asked, leaning closer.

"Y-yours, my liege."

"What's wrong at home?" the king's voice cracked. "Is it my mother?"

"No, sir, she is drumming up more support for you in other islands of Freng. It's your brother."

The king leaned back, whiskers stiffening. "Go on."

The other soldiers had all stopped drinking and the messenger seemed acutely aware of all the eyes on him.

"Your brother is also facing a siege of sorts. Peasants are revolting against him. He's raised the taxes."

Ridgerd unsheathed his sword, a reflex that horrified Jab. "What?"

"I-I'm sorry, King Ridgerd." The messenger backed away, palms raised.

Jab's eyes widened. Ridgerd would have to leave Qawar and deal with this. He almost shouted out a prayer of thanks in front of everyone, though the idea that it took innocent rodents suffering somewhere else to bring this out calmed Jab's enthusiasm.

"The prince has jailed seedlings who spoke against him. The commoners are begging for your return."

"And how do you know this, messenger?" Ridgerd asked.

The mole rat's gaze fell to his hindpaws. "Emperor Rattarossa has a network of spies. Word came to Kraksnout Castle, and this message was meant to go to him. But after watching him slaughter all those prisoners, I-I couldn't, good king."

"'Good king.'" Ridgerd shook his head. "I thank you for bringing this to me. If you've double-crossed Rattarossa, you are safer with me. Join us."

Jab was so delighted at Ridgerd's misfortune that he felt guilty. But how could he not? He'd been praying, begging for some peaceful solution. Ridgerd would go home with his soldiers to discipline his brother, and Rattarossa would be overwhelmed. Nothing could be better.

Ridgerd lifted his sword over his head. "Lads, I hate to ask this of you, but I know the All-Planter will reward us. We must double our efforts to reach the Holy City. We must liberate the city so we can complete our pilgrimage and return home. Those are your wives and children suffering under my brother. We will make things right. To Olihort!"

"To Olihort!" came the chorus.

Jab's whiskers drooped under the weight of his incorrect assumptions. Instead of giving up, Ridgerd would just fight harder.

21

SANU

"The Barkhearts? I don't doubt their conviction and devotion to Ganan, but I have heard unsettling rumors. I've served two Saplings in the Holy City, and both kept that order at tail's length. Wisely, I think."

- The only off-topic thing Whima said on their ride out of ZelZaytun

Sanu covered his eyes against the torrent of sand east of ZelZaytun. The harsh desert contrasted against the lush vegetation to the south and west of the city. The prayer warden had explained once that the island had these two extremes to show the duality of rodents or something, but Sanu had only half-listened when they were in the prayer hall. He did like when the prayer wardens said that even animals as fierce as scavenging hyenas were part of the

All-Planter's creation, though ancient rodents feared them as evil spirits.

But Sanu knew one thing for sure, he and Whima were going in the direction of Rattin, his hometown, and Vermitch was as reliable as ever. The road was hard, and Whima wasn't the conversationalist that Brouglas and Yagub were, and definitely not Ridgerd. The prospect of seeing Ridgerd again made Sanu tense—the king might see him as a traitor. "Are you positive the king is going this way?"

"Scouts spotted banners in this direction," Whima replied. "Common sense dictates that the faster force would go the way of the west coast, and the force with siege equipment would go through the arid zone."

Sanu remembered Ridgerd's love of battering rams. He definitely would've taken the hotter, drier route. He hoped Rattarossa got stuck in the mud on the other side of the island.

A few minutes passed until Sanu noticed some specks on the horizon over a sandy hill. Squinting, he recognized the banner and colors.

A crowned bear in dazzling gold.

This wasn't Ridgerd's force. This was Rattarossa's. Cladh or Whima had made an awful mistake.

"We have to turn around," Sanu said. "That's not Ridgerd."

"No." Whima's voice was matter-of-fact. "My instructions were to give the message to whichever king we found, and found a king we have. You are under the Sapling's protection. You are safe."

Nobody was safe around Rattarossa. The banners disappeared on the other side of the hill, and somehow not knowing their precise location made Sanu want to shriek. That crafty emperor would do anything to gain more power, and Rattin wasn't too far away.

Whima urged Vermitch to gallop faster, which kicked up dust and sand along the road.

The thought of meeting that hulking bearded dormouse again made Sanu shiver in the saddle. "I don't think he'll recognize me, but I'll disguise my voice when we talk to him."

"We won't risk it." Whima nudged him. "I'll deliver the message to Rattarossa myself. You can watch the horse."

Even though the delivery was flat, Sanu could tell that was about as close as Whima got to compassion. "Thanks," Sanu muttered.

After a few more minutes, they passed the dune, and sparse grass defied the sands, along with the occasional stubborn tree. As long as they followed this road, they would reach Rattin. As would Rattarossa's force, which included the Barkhearts.

"There's a small town up ahead," Sanu said. "They're in danger."

"No," Whima replied. "Nasalid knew the invaders would feed off the towns, so he emptied them all between the Holy City and Kraksnout. Rattin, Sqirlib, Banuj, and the villages are all empty houses now. Most were taken into ZelZaytun. Others are taking temporary refuge on the neighboring islands."

After being away from Rattin for so long, Sanu wished he could return to the town and see it as it was meant to be, with his friends running around between the shops, the adults haggling with the traders who'd pass through, and even the call to prayer. But it would be silent and empty now.

They neared the town, and Sanu got a full view of Rattarossa's troops. The force was bigger than Sanu had remembered. There were enough soldiers to assemble all types of siege weapons and enough camp followers to support a city. Sitting as straight as possible, Sanu got a view of the prayer hall, the tallest building in Rattin.

He remembered the last time a large group of Sprouter knights came here. Nasalid put them to the torch, and it had separated Sanu from Jab. Sanu's salvation had come in the form of the knight outside the fire, Sir Brouglas. Sanu wondered what Brouglas would think about the image of Rattarossa's warriors descending on the town now.

Sanu pointed past the troops and town to the two rocky formations outside town. Everyone called them Rattin's "horns," but they were more like rocky spikes than anything else. "Whima, take the long way around and get us behind the horns. We'll be able to see and hear them before they notice us." Sanu didn't want to admit that the horns would also give him a place to hide if things went poorly.

Galloping toward the horns, they kept quiet, keeping an eye on Rattarossa's force encircling Rattin's hopefully empty buildings. "I promise you are safe," Whima murmured. "I represent the Holy City's Sapling. Attacking me would be attacking her, which no Sprouter in their right mind would do. She is a living beacon of Lord Ganan, Blest be Him."

The image of Grovekeeper prisoners being flung over Kraksnout's walls flashed in Sanu's head. Rattarossa didn't seem too concerned with what was proper. "Please be careful."

Vermitch climbed the mesa leading to Rattin's horns, and Rattarossa's fighters crisscrossed the town. The fact that they weren't dragging any of Sanu's friends or their parents out of the houses was a good sign, but the grunts he could hear from them didn't carry a happy overtone.

Atop the hill, Sanu and Whima dismounted, and Sanu grabbed Vermitch's reins. Rattarossa was shouting at his soldiers. Since he was speaking Rottelander, Sanu didn't catch a word, but the tone was clear enough. Sanu peeked around the rocky horn, glancing below. Most of the soldiers wore the Barkheart Order armor, and a pair of them ignited torches.

In broad daylight.

Flames near Rattin had nearly killed Sanu and Jab a few months ago. The stench of burning fur. The screams. Sanu closed his eyes and shook his head. There was no reason to burn down Rattin. Thankfully, this was when Whima arrived, brandishing the rolled-up message with Cladh's Sapling seal. He and the king exchanged words in Rottelander, and Sanu wished he'd spent as much time learning that as he did Frenglese. Some of the words sounded the same, but with the different accents, Sanu couldn't be sure of anything.

After a brief exchange, Whima rolled up his message. Rattarossa pointed to one of the Barkheart knights who carried a devilbeak.

Whima looked from side to side, and Sanu wished he were close enough to see his expression beyond twitching whiskers. Two soldiers came up from behind Whima and grabbed him.

Then Whima switched languages to Frenglese. "No! You can't do this!"

The devilbeak-wielding knight approached Whima, weapon held high.

Sanu couldn't watch. He jumped back on Vermitch and galloped away, but the sound of Vermitch's hoofbeats didn't muffle Whima's last scream.

22

JAB

Lord Ganan, Blest be You, sometimes I worry about how much wrong I've done. It's so hard for me to move on from my faults. Years later, and I'm plagued by individual moments of nastiness. I will make it my life's work to become a better version of myself. You are the stake which I can grow around.

- *From the prayer journal of Sir Brouglas*

Jab nudged Brouglas in the saddle. "Careful, there's an axe on the ground." Jab pointed to a discarded wood chopping axe, plonked in the carpet of dried leaves.

Brouglas steered the horse around the tool. "Who would forget an axe like that?"

"There are others." Yagub lifted it up and showed it to the king. "My liege, what do you think of this?"

Without breaking his stride, the royal hamster smirked. "These woodcutters hurried. They didn't pick the trees carefully at all or replant new saplings."

Jab debated using this opportunity to mention how confusing it was to use the word "sapling" as a title for someone in their religion and use it to refer to a tree in normal conversation, but kept quiet. He and Sanu would laugh about it later.

"Siege engines for Kraksnout?" Brouglas offered.

"Perhaps," the king mused. "Or for arrows."

Jab thought it could be for warships too, but didn't want to give them any clues. "I think what matters is that they knew you were coming."

King Ridgerd nodded toward Jab. "The woodcutters and craftsrodents of Qawar have nothing to fear from us as long as they keep their distance and don't interfere."

Jab glared. Nobody should fear him since he shouldn't be here. He tried to think of a way to mention Ridgerd's brother back in Freng, but couldn't figure out how to do it naturally. Returning home early without fighting had to be Ridgerd's own idea.

They continued marching through the chopped forest, stepping over other forgotten and abandoned tools, twigs, and crumpled leaves. All the armored hindpaws and hooves crunching through the leaves made more noise than the biggest waves on the open seas.

Nobody in ZelZaytun could possibly be unsure about where they were. Jab gazed at the holy tree in the distance. For so long, he'd kept himself from looking at it, since it had been under foreign occupation. Now that he was free to look at it again, he wondered if he'd be witness to the tree's grove coming into foreigner paws, making Nasalid's victory meaningless.

As sunset approached, Jab wondered how he could tell Brouglas that he needed to pray, as if he hadn't insulted the beaver enough with his lies about wanting to become a Sprouter.

King Ridgerd whistled, and an unseen trumpeter blew a toot. The horde of soldiers and camp followers ground to a halt. Brouglas dismounted the horse and tapped Jab's knee. "You'll probably be wanting to pray, won't you? We're camping for the night."

Jab *did* want to pray the All-Planter would change Ridgerd's mind and send him home.

The king helped the injured soldier riding his horse dismount. "Young Jab, when you complete your prayer, see me in my tent." It was a command, and Jab debated reminding Ridgerd that he wasn't Jab's king, but Jab wouldn't miss this opportunity to get in the king's round ear about returning home.

As the others prepared tents and campfires, Jab cleared a space in the leaves for himself, thankful these Sprouters respected him enough to let him do this, even if they didn't respect him enough to cancel the invasion. He bowed and began his evening prayers, remembering first Sanu, then their parents, and brave Kash, Jab's mentor. He even prayed for Brouglas, Yagub, and all the other Sprouters here. Jab needed a miracle.

All of Qawar did. Maybe the rainy season would start early and rust all their weapons while they weren't paying attention.

Jab gazed upon the holy tree, made even more of a majestic sight by the setting sun casting a spotlight on it. Jab had spent so many nights in Rattin dancing in the speckled moonlight, since the tree covered the moon for a few months out of the year, and only trickles of silver moonbeams snuck between the branches and leaves high in the sky.

Hoping the All-Planter would soothe his anguish, Jab completed his prayers and approached Ridgerd's tent. Even though he hadn't watched anyone pitch it, the decorations made it obvious that it was the king's. Jab remembered Nasalid's layers of trickery to conceal which tent was his, and had half a mind to warn Ridgerd not to broadcast where he was to everyone, but again, he didn't want to give an invader advice.

A soldier blocked the entrance with a spear, but lifted it for Jab. "The king's expecting you," he said in a gruff accent.

Jab wasn't sure how to respond politely, so he nodded and entered.

The inside was less lavish than Jab had expected, but it still boasted royal trappings like a weapons rack and a map table, which Ridgerd sat at. "There he is," Ridgerd said. "Welcome. Back on Coppergrass, your brother gave me quite the game of double siege. I'd like to play you, since all the other soldiers in camp have run out of ways to lose to me." He cast a wide and charming grin. "My cook is making us some loov, using the Mulcher from Coppergrass's recipe. No olives."

"Thank you." Jab didn't want to eat with the king at all, but he needed to get him talking.

Ridgerd placed an oak box the size of Jab's forearm on the table. He opened it and displayed the double siege set inside.

"I'm not much of a player, King Ridgerd." Jab waved his paw dismissively. "That was more of Sanu's passion."

"Come, sit," Ridgerd insisted. "One game." He plucked out the red and blue general pieces. "You can pick the color and the first player."

"Sanu told me your strategy," Jab said, still standing. "You lead with your general piece. It's a trap for the other player. They don't expect such a bold move and get sloppy. It's why you fight in the front too. I watched that happen outside Sqirlib."

Ridgerd leaned back, pulling out the siege engine and villager pieces. "You think you know what I'll do. So you suppose you can beat me then?"

This was Jab's chance. "No. Since I know you play double siege like you fight, playing you would be like watching you rehearse killing Grovekeepers. That's not a game I want to be a part of."

Ridgerd's eyes widened, but he didn't seem angry. Instead, he twirled a blue vanguard piece between his fingers. "I imagine that *would* be difficult emotionally."

"That's not all," Jab said. "That messenger said the rodents in your kingdom are suffering under your brother. It's bad enough knowing you're going to kill Grovekeepers, but to do that while your own rodents are starving is too upsetting for me to want to move pieces around a board. I'm sorry I can't be more entertaining."

Ridgerd's stony expression turned into a scowl. "We are here as pilgrims. I don't know how many times you need to hear that. Now, go and rest up. We have an assault tomorrow."

Jab glanced at the map of Qawar laid out on Ridgerd's cot. They couldn't attack ZelZaytun, but there was one other target Ridgerd had within a day's journey. The lake south of ZelZaytun had a supply depot, originally used by the Frengs under Lady Marjitay. Jab had found it while scouting and been present for the battle in which Nasalid took it over. Ridgerd was about to do the same precise thing Nasalid had before.

Jab would have to physically return to the place he visited in his nightmares each night, since he'd failed with the king.

23

SANU

I have good news for General Ironseed, but I worry it won't fix his foul mood. Apparently, there's an independent island that the Frengs and Rottelanders have fought over for decades. I think it's called Frunkenbarg or something. The ruler died with no heir. That will get hairy in a few years, mark my words.

- Diaries of General Ironseed's secretary

Galloping away from the horns of Rattin, Sanu wondered if the phrase "Don't kill the messenger," ever made it to Rotteland. Cringing, he knew it certainly had, but it didn't matter to Rattarossa or the Barkheart knights. He hated himself for watching from afar as Whima died with the copy of Cladh's message meant for Rattarossa, a plea to turn around and abandon the invasion. Sanu wondered if that meant Cladh was in danger from this guy and his soldiers as much as Nasalid was.

A year ago, Sanu would've never dreamed of abandoning Nasalid after getting a chance to be in ZelZaytun with him. He should've listened to his old self. He thundered toward the city, desperate to beg for forgiveness, with nothing to show for his escape besides saying, "Rattarossa is just as bad as everyone says he is. Maybe worse."

As the sacred tree grew in the distance, Sanu gazed upon it, straining his neck and still unable to see the top. Low-hanging clouds obscured it. When the city walls came into view, Sanu slowed Vermitch to a halt. Cladh needed to know that Whima had died in her service, but Nasalid also needed something.

Nasalid had already known that one of the armies would approach Rattin, but telling him they'd arrived didn't feel like enough. He had to know Rattarossa's next move if he wanted to get in the Liberator's good graces. Sanu stared at the tree, hoping for some sign from the All-Planter.

He wasn't sure what he expected, but sunset came, illuminating the Gnaverwood from behind, and it seemed like its trunk glowed with the reddening sunlight.

Red like Rattarossa's beard.

Sanu urged Vermitch to turn around, and he headed down the trade road back toward Rattin's horns. From there, he'd have a better vantage point.

After spending so much time poring over maps with Ridgerd and earlier in life with Dad, Sanu had Qawar's geography memorized. From

Rattin, one could head west to ZelZaytun, north to Kraksnout, east to Banuj and the other trading ports, or south to ZelZaytun's lake. He bet Rattarossa would go east and rampage across the rest of Qawar, but he had to be sure. He wished Jab were with him and could offer some scouting advice.

Coming up to the horns, Vermitch stomped on something metallic. Sanu slowed down to peer at it. It was a metal shield, kite-shaped with a raised part in the middle in the shape of Ganan's Rake. Some weeds held it in place. Sanu dismounted and pulled it from the ground. He hadn't noticed it before. It must've been dropped by a knight in the Battle of Rattin's Horns, the one that separated Sanu and Jab the first time.

Pushing the weeds and dirt off, it surprised Sanu how nature could reclaim what war had stolen. Its protection also might be the difference between life and death if one of those Barkheart monsters found him. Sanu hopped back on Vermitch, finding his balance a bit more difficult with the kite shield strapped to his back.

Rattarossa's horde was on the move, leaving Rattin, which was a huge relief. Those torches he'd seen before had made him nervous.

The army returned to the road which cut Rattin into fourths, and went south. Sanu's eyes widened. South?

They weren't here to plunder the trading ports. They wanted to weaken ZelZaytun. Nasalid had done the same thing by taking over that lake. Jab had been witness to the battle that took place there, and even though he didn't talk about it much, Sanu knew it still gave his twin nightmares. Real battles were no place for young squirrels, but he'd lost count of how many he and Jab had seen, and they weren't even teenagers yet.

Sanu wondered if anyone cared how the war affected kids.

He waited until the whole force had funneled into the south road, and readied to return to ZelZaytun with the news. When he turned around, two mounted Barkheart Order knights greeted him. One wielded a devilbeak and the other a bow.

Heart racing, Sanu tried to think of what Jab would do.

The archer growled something at him in Rottelander, and Sanu had no idea how to respond.

The other soldier spoke in Frenglese. "What is your business here?"

They must've seen Sanu's new shield. Sanu sucked in a deep breath. "Serenity to your family!" He knew he shouldn't have expected them to reply with "tranquility to your home," but a greeting was a greeting and the phrase gave him some confidence. "My father was a knight sworn to Lady Marjitay. I found out he died in the battle that was here a few months ago. I came to get his shield."

Both knights exchanged a glance, but with their helmet visors, Sanu couldn't see their expression. "A Qawari squirrel served the Honking Goose?"

Sanu had forgotten about that nickname for her. Even though she was a mole rat, she sure squawked and acted like a goose. "Yes," Sanu replied. "Many squirrels on Qawar are Sprouters and many are Mulchers."

"Where are you going?" the archer demanded in a heavy accent.

"Back home," Sanu said. That wouldn't be good enough. "My mother is grieving." In that moment, he gained a new appreciation for Jab's ability to lie to save his life.

The other soldier trotted forward, his horse wearing a matching set of armor and moving just as stiffly as Sanu had expected. "We need a donation," he said. "To fund our cleansing of this island."

Cleansing? Sanu fought the urge to spit at them. "I-I don't have any money. I need to return my father's shield to my mother. We don't have anything to remember him by."

The archer grabbed an arrow from the quiver attached to his saddle. "You will tell her how you assisted the Barkheart Order and helped Emperor Rattarossa restore Sprouter rule to the holy island. How you are a part of the story of our hero."

That wasn't exactly something they could eat. Sanu gripped Vermitch's reins tighter. If he gave them his shield, they could shoot him in the back. Sanu watched the knights with torches place them against Rattin's wood buildings.

Some hero Rattarossa was.

With a final glance at the other horses' heavy armor, Sanu kicked Vermitch into a sudden gallop, taking a sharp turn to the right, where he knew the rocks were looser.

"Hey!" a soldier shouted. They galloped after him, but Vermitch was faster without the armor.

Sanu charged away from them, making a tight turn and heading toward ZelZaytun. A whinnying neigh from behind told him one of the horses got stuck in the gravel. Sanu didn't dare look over his shoulder. He had to keep pushing ahead.

After a solid minute of galloping, he heard a *fhwit* sound from behind, followed by a metallic *thunk* against the kite shield. The archer had fired, and the shield had saved his life. Vermitch whinnied, and Sanu urged him faster. "Come on," he begged the horse. "We'll be home soon." Approaching the Holy City, Sanu knew it was the horse's home, not his.

Distant smoke tickled Sanu's nostrils, tempting the tears forming in his eyes.

Sanu's only home was engulfed in Rattarossa's fire, and a dead squirrel's plea for peace burned with it.

24

JAB

When Ganan arrived at Banuj to rest His hindpaws, a funeral procession marched by. One of Ganan's followers noticed how many weeping Mulchers were yanking twigs from their beards and crying out in anguish. The follower scoffed, saying, "Lord, look how dramatic they are. Don't they know whoever died is now in the All-Planter's embrace?" Ganan placed His Rake in the dirt and scratched an X. He stood in the middle and declared, "Do not insult those who weep for a lost loved one. Let their hearts feel the emotion as much as you let their minds understand their loved one's suffering has ended. Blessed be they who keep mind and heart in balance." From that spot, a cedar grows to this day.

- Excerpt from the Ganandeeds,
"The Funeral at Banuj"

With the sunrise and his prayers completed, a hopeful Jab picked at the breakfast he'd brought to his secluded spot in the camp. Ridgerd's troops and camp followers all attended their Offering Meal ritual service. Jab respected individual Sprouters, but the idea of eating olives in the sight of the holy tree made him uneasy. They deserved to eat them as much as Grovekeepers deserved to not eat them.

How could these pilgrims not understand that Nasalid wanted all faiths practiced freely? Politicians grubbing their paws and playing at empire building—the whole enterprise made Jab lose his appetite. He forced down his grains and pistachios, and packed his few things together. He wouldn't have much time before they finished their ritual and would set out again. Jab breathed deep, trying not to focus too much on the crumpling leaves under his hindpaws.

Knowing they would be at the lake depot soon, the crunch of dead plants took Jab's mind to a dark memory of crunching bones not too far from here. Nasalid had attacked the hidden lake depot used by Lady Marjitay to supply her troops. Even though outnumbered, Lady Marjitay's soldiers fought bravely, and Jab saw firstpaw how effective heavy armor was. Each soldier was a fortress unto himself, and it took teams of Nasalid's troops with clubs to act like battering rams and bring them down. It was a gory display, and Jab hated how often he returned to that lake in his nightmares.

Now he was returning in the fur.

Jab shook his head at the thought and met up with Brouglas and Yagub outside Brouglas's tent.

"How were your prayers?" Brouglas asked Jab with sincerity.

Jab didn't know how to tell him that was a weird question since he knew the old beaver was just being polite. "Good. I prayed for your safety. Sanu's too."

"What, not mine?" Yagub chuckled.

Jab shrugged. "That's between me and the All-Planter."

"Ha!" The laugh came from King Ridgerd. Jab was shocked he didn't hear him coming. "You can take that as a 'no,' Yagub. Young Jab, I understand you've been to this lake before. How muddy is it at this time of year? Will our horses and wagons get stuck?"

Jab's mouth dried. He needed to lie. Tell Ridgerd to go on hindpaw. That would give Nasalid's garrison at the lake depot a chance to run away.

"No," Yagub said. "We have a few more weeks before the rains really get going."

Ridgerd arched an eyebrow. "Thank you. Sir Brouglas, you've been around these parts. What other terrain can we expect?"

Jab had missed his chance. He stared at his hindpaws.

Brouglas placed an arm around Jab. "My liege, Jab was present at the battle that took place at the lake. He was too young to see such a thing. Frankly, he's too young to see much of what he already has. It's not fair to ask him about it. But to your question, I never made it around the lake. I trust Yagub's opinion."

Jab met the royal hamster's gaze. "The lake is home to geese. They will give away your position if you try an ambush." A harmless goose's death was first in that battle. He couldn't look at a bird without remembering the reddened feathers.

Ridgerd nodded. "Then goose will be on the menu."

The goose's awful death-honk from the battle rang in Jab's ears. "No. I watched someone make that mistake. The geese make lots of noise when they're killed. You're better off not getting too close to the waters."

"Sage counsel." Ridgerd tousled Jab's head hair and nodded at Yagub. "This is why I brought you two along." After a deep inhale, he turned to his soldiers and lifted his sword up high. "All right lads, we're heading out. Expect resistance at the lake. If you kill one of the local geese, I'll tell the seedlings to cut you off from the holy olives. Understood?"

"Yes, good King Ridgerd!" the soldiers chorused as if they'd rehearsed the response. It seemed like a far cry from the soldiers on Coppergrass Island who thought the king was some kind of repulsive sinner who they wanted nothing to do with. Maybe seeing him in battle up close and comparing him to Rattarossa was enough to change their minds.

The host moved out, heading southeast toward the lake. Once Jab sat in Brouglas's saddle, the Gnaverwood's shadow passed over him. Within a few steps, the shadow had swallowed him up like a blanket.

Jab recited verses from the Divine Poetics in his head, straining to remember each portion of the holy text, particularly the ones about dealing with anxiety and fear. He had been strong on Coppergrass when it was just him and Brouglas. Sanu survived the battle on Rattin's horns because of Brouglas's heroics. The beaver knight's presence meant everything was survivable. Jab hadn't been with him during the first battle at the lake, so this time would be different.

And maybe he'd get lucky and the lake garrison would be so overwhelmingly powerful that Ridgerd's troops would turn tail and run, or the opposite would happen. Either way, Jab prayed that no more blood would stain Qawar's soil.

When Jab figured they were halfway to the lake, he noticed a road splintering off theirs. If he remembered his maps correctly, it would lead to a trading port. And a port meant ships to take these soldiers back to Freng.

Jab spoke a bit more loudly than he needed to. "Sir Brouglas, how do you think my brother is faring? I'm anxious to see him again."

Out of the corner of his eye, Jab noticed King Ridgerd glance over at him.

Without waiting for Brouglas to respond, Jab continued. "We've just been through so much, both together and apart. He's the only family I have."

Sir Brouglas sighed. "I'm sure he's well. Sanu is a crafty boy. If Lady Marjitay didn't chop off his head, he can talk his way out of anything. He's crafty and kind, much like his brother."

Jab appreciated the kind words but that wasn't the reaction he needed. "I've started reading your prayer journal like you asked. Have you heard from your brother lately?"

The beaver shifted in the saddle. "I suppose you haven't gotten to that part of my prayer journal. Relationships with siblings are complicated."

Jab's heart plummeted. He didn't want to force Brouglas to relive any painful family drama. Brouglas was supposed to say something like, "Of course, I love my brother, who happens to have the same name as Ridgerd's brother. Say, oh good king, my liege Ridgerd, don't you want to see your brother back home in Freng where it's not so hot?"

Maybe Jab should've written it down for him.

Instead, Brouglas continued. "My older brother was my role model. I spent so much of my life trying to be him. I trained with a sword because he did. I read because he did. I learned Rottelander and Mausfjorder to impress him. And as adults, I'm sad to say we grew apart. I have sent him letters. If you've been reading my journal, you're probably sick of me mentioning him."

Brouglas sniffed. "His responses were sporadic. Maybe every fifth one got a reply for a few years, but then nothing. I have spent so much time wondering what I could have done differently to make him still want to be a brother to me. I wish I knew."

"I-I'm sorry I said anything, Brouglas," Jab said. "I have been reading your journal like you said. I should have known to keep quiet."

"It's fine, lad," Brouglas replied, with a tiny crack in his voice. "I wish we weren't brothers divided. And I wish I knew why we were divided. I'm torn between respecting his decision to live his life without me and to keep reaching out, letting him know I never forgot him. After all this, he's still my brother."

The king watched them. This wasn't what Jab had wanted.

Yagub scoffed, surprising Jab. He'd forgotten he was there beside them in the procession. "You're better off without him. He sounds like an awful brother. You've got brothers-in-arms, which is better."

King Ridgerd sidestepped in his march to join them. "Jab, I promise we'll get you and Sanu reunited. If I fail, know that it was not from lack of trying. Sir Brouglas, I didn't know you had a brother. Yours sounds a bit like mine."

Jab curled his tail tight. This was his chance. "There's a port not too far from here, King Ridgerd. You could send everyone home and go deal with your brother. You could make amends with him."

The hamster glanced over his shoulder in the road's direction. "That will be the port from which we send the news of our victory then. I'll prepare a message after the battle is over."

Yagub pointed ahead. "Chimney smoke! We're close to the depot."

Jab examined the terrain. The last time he was here, the lake was surrounded by trees to the point where it was nearly hidden. But the lake sat before them, and it was hidden, not by trees, but grass. All the trees had been cut down here too.

Nasalid's deforestation of Qawar was almost as unsettling as the king's determination to plow forward. Another tear fell on Jab's shoulder.

At least Jab had succeeded in forgetting about the horrors of the last lake battle.

25

SANU

"Rattarossa made offers to the mayors of the port towns. Take arms against Nasalid and enjoy his protection."

"That's ridiculous. The blood has barely dried from where Nasalid spilled Freng blood to save them."

"Money helps rodents forget. I bet he said he'd protect them from Ridgerd too."

"You don't need to pay me to take protection against him."

- Overheard chatter at the ZelZaytun guardhouse

Sanu was panting so hard he could barely answer the gatekeeper's questions.

"I ... saw ... Ratta ... rossa's army. He ... torched R-r—" Sanu winced hard. He couldn't get the name out. Somehow, holding in Rattin's name kept it alive and intact somehow.

"Rattin?" the armored gatekeeper asked, shifting in his armor. "Emperor Rattarossa reached Rattin and set it aflame?"

"I told you he's a monster," another gatekeeper said.

Sanu nodded, blinking hard to push away the tears forming on his eyelids. Breathing deep, he forced composure. "Let me inside. I need to tell Nasalid where he's heading."

The second gatekeeper leaned over, sizing up Sanu's bushy tail. "Are you from Rattin, boy?"

Sanu couldn't fight the tears this time. "Yes. Nasalid agreed to take me and my brother in."

"You're Sanu!"

That stopped the tears. "W-what? How did you know?"

The first guard raised his fist and the wrought iron gate lifted with a series of *racka-clicks*, like a giant metal crossbow being cranked. "The Liberator sent out search parties to find you. We've been on alert for a brown squirrel your age. He was worried."

Sanu's jaw hung open. As much as Nasalid had to worry about, he'd wasted time searching for Sanu. While Sanu had been lamenting his loss of a physical home, someone else was worried about him. The guilt weighed in his stomach. "Um, can you take me to him?"

The second guard shook his head. "We can take you to the Sapling. Nasalid had to ride out to one of the forward bases with a battalion and supplies to the force laying siege to Kraksnout."

With a *thunk*, the gate finished rising, and the guards ushered Sanu inside. He tugged the reins and Vermitch clopped forward. As he traversed the streets of ZelZaytun with the guard, he explained what had happened to Rattin and Whima, all while scanning for signs of a Rattin citizen living in the city.

But as they left the Grovekeeper quarter for the Sprouter one, he accepted the fact that the city was too big with too many rodents for him to luck into one. At least he'd see Cladh.

Outside the grand Gananhall steps, a jird in a fancy thobe argued with someone dressed like a seedling. Between them, a red squirrel with Mulcher twigs in his beard gestured to both of them.

The guard cleared his throat as they approached. "Dilaal, I present to you Sanu of Rattin." He turned to Sanu and gestured toward the jird. "This is Dilaal, mayor of ZelZaytun and brother of Nasalid the Liberator."

"*Appointed* mayor," the Mulcher said, tugging at the end of his long beard.

Dilaal shot him a glare then approached Sanu. "Sanu of Rattin, I'm sorry I didn't meet with you earlier." His voice sounded like Nasalid's if it had never been tempered in the fire of war and his younger, unscarred face resembled Nasalid's if he'd never been in a fight. "My brother was panicked over your disappearance." He scowled over his shoulder at the seedling. "Especially once he found out that the Sapling sponsored your trip."

"I-I'm sorry," Sanu stuttered. "I thought I had an opportunity to get one of the invader kings to retreat from the island. The Sprouters respect Saplings."

Dilaal crossed his arms and made a circle in the street with his whip of a tail. "Is that why you've returned? To announce that one of the war mongers no longer thirsts for blood and went home with his apologies?"

Even though Sanu was atop a horse, he felt smaller than everyone else there. "No. Rattarossa killed Cladh's bodyguard because of his message and then burned Rattin down."

The Mulcher shook his head and the seedling gasped. Dilaal extended a paw, offering to help Sanu off the saddle. "Monstrous. But sometimes in double siege, you must sacrifice a piece to gain insight into your enemy's plans."

Sanu accepted the help with one paw and clenched the other in a fist. Rattin wasn't a game piece to be sacrificed.

Once Sanu was down, Dilaal turned to the others. "We know now what *won't* work against Rattarossa and what happened to the first messenger. If the second messenger doesn't return from King Ridgerd, we'll know the hearts of both our enemies."

The seedling approached Sanu, eyes on the ground. "When they killed Whima, were they fast? Did he suffer?" The crack in his voice made Sanu wonder what their relationship was.

Sanu tried to explain what happened without replaying the image or hearing the sound again in his mind. "They used a devilbeak. It only took one hit."

"Th-thank you," the seedling replied. "I will inform the Sapling of the bravery of you both." His voice hardened and he gazed up at Dilaal. "*After* someone explains why he ordered an entire forest chopped down without agreement from the council."

The Mulcher nodded, and Sanu wished he remembered all the terms for the long robes and headwraps he wore. "You and your brother are cutting too many trees. Animals are leaving if not outright dying."

Dilaal scoffed. "I'd prefer a dead tree to a dead citizen of ZelZaytun any day. It would be nice if the foreign Sprouters stopped attacking, and then we wouldn't need to worry about arrows and warships."

Sanu came between the three of them. "Hey, hey, we're all on the same side, aren't we?"

The guard muttered under his breath, "Bad move, kid."

The Mulcher patted Sanu on the back. "You can always trust a squirrel to speak honestly."

"Yes," Dilaal said. "We can continue this discussion another time. After the war, we'll import seeds and young trees to replenish the island. Sanu, you must join me to tell the garrison chiefs what you learned."

Sanu gazed at the Gananhall. He wished Cladh were here. Looking at the seedling, he asked, "Would you take this horse back to Cladh? She's been taking care of it. And, um, could you tell her I'm sorry about Whima?"

The seedling replied with a sad smile. "Of course."

Sanu followed Dilaal back toward the city's center.

"That must have been an awful experience, watching a good rodent die like that," the jird said. "We'll get justice for him. And your town. Once I can send a message to my brother that you're safe, we'll learn what you know and find a way to get these invaders off Qawar for good."

It wasn't what Sanu wanted to hear, and the idea of Qawar losing its trees did not sit well, but at least there was progress.

26

JAB

In one of your sermons, when someone asked you how many times to forgive another rodent, you said that one hundred and eleven times would still not be enough. I haven't counted, but I feel like I've forgiven my brother one hundred and twelve times. I almost wrote "Now what?" but I suppose I instead must pray for the strength to keep forgiving, since I know the All-Planter does not have a limit. Please, my lord, watch over my brother.

- *From the prayer journal of Sir Brouglas*

No progress had been made.

A single hill separated Jab and Ridgerd's horde from ZelZaytun on their left. The Gnaverwood couldn't be hidden, but the hill rose just high enough to obscure the city walls.

Jab hadn't been this close since he left Qawar to meet Ridgerd for the first time.

On their right lay the lake from Jab's nightmares, no longer hidden by trees and probably no longer home to innocent geese. The lack of trees made the place easier to stomach, since the only constant between the last battle and now was the supply buildings. Last time, a pawful of heavily armored knights stood their ground and wreaked havoc on Nasalid's light troops. It had taken dozens to overwhelm five. And as close as they were, Jab should have spotted some of Nasalid's troops by now.

"Looks deserted, my king," Brouglas called.

"Aye, but it could be a trap," the royal hamster replied.

Yagub scoffed. "They knew we were coming and hightailed it back to the city. Your reputation precedes you, Ridgerd Steelfur!"

Jab rolled his eyes, and noticed the sunlight had faded.

"Archers in the hills!" a soldier called.

Jab checked over his right shoulder, and saw a torrent of arrows descending on them.

"Shields!" Ridgerd roared. "Take cover!"

In one motion, Sir Brouglas lifted his kite shield from the side of the saddle and shoved Jab off the horse.

Jab rolled off, hunkering behind Brouglas's horse. The arrows smacked into the soldiers' helmets and shields like dropped knives onto sheet metal. Behind him, camp rodents and horses dropped where they stood. When the downpour of sharpened steel ended, Jab glanced over the horse.

"Are you hurt?" Brouglas asked. "I worried my shield couldn't protect you."

"We're fine." Yagub lowered his shield, pointing at the hill. "They've taken position up there!"

"To arms, lads!" Ridgerd called. The king moved the lifeless body of the soldier who'd been riding his horse onto the ground in a movement that was both swift and gentle. Snarling, he mounted his armored steed, lifted his sword, and bellowed, "Take that hill and avenge our fallen! Trust your armor again!"

Another cloud of arrows darkened the sky, and Ridgerd lowered his shield to cover his horse, ducking his head under it. A V-formation of mounted knights trailed behind him, with men-at-arms bringing up the rear.

Like before, Brouglas stayed behind. "Tend to the wounded, Yagub."

The squirrel grimaced. "You won't let me in on the fun."

The shrieks of injured rodents filled the air. "War isn't fun," Jab hissed.

He crawled over to the fallen soldier Ridgerd had been letting ride his horse. Jab hadn't come this close to a dead squirrel since he'd prepared his parents for their funeral. Anguish froze in the rodent's eyes. Jab checked for signs of breathing, but it seemed like the arrow was savage and surgical.

Around him, scores of soldiers writhed, with arrows sticking out of their legs and chests. Their deaths might be prevented. On the hill, at least a dozen of Ridgerd's soldiers lost their footing, stumbling down the hill while the archers rained arrows on them. Jab couldn't watch. He headed to the closest injured soldier so he might save his life or pray with him. Any kind of mercy he could give would be better than standing around.

But as the *thwang-thwang-thwang* of hundreds of archers releasing arrows slowed, Jab's curiosity overpowered his fear. Ridgerd had connected with the first line of archers and leapt off his horse, mowing down Nasalid's troops who were within reach of his large sword. The others scurried away, taking up new positions.

A nearby moan made Jab refocus and kneel among the fallen, where a soldier with an arrow in his chest squirmed. Jab gently removed his helmet.

"You'll be all right," Jab soothed. "We'll get you to a seedling, and—"

"N-no, boy. Sit me up straight. Everything is g-going dark. Let me see the Gnaverwood."

Jab's eyes widened and his paws grew shaky. "Of course." He heaved the unarmored soldier to a seated position and turned his torso toward the holy olive tree.

"It's magnificent," he whispered. "It's like I can see the entry to the Walled Garden. Th-thank you, boy." The soldier coughed, wheezed, and slumped back to the ground.

When Jab buried his parents, he and Sanu chose a hill so they'd be in view of that same holy tree.

Halfway up the hill, Ridgerd had penetrated through to the second line of archers, which was buckling faster than the first. Fewer Sprouter soldiers were with him, and more were stumbling down the hill, tripping up those who were trying to join their king.

Jab moved toward the next fallen rodent, careful not to trip on the scattered arrows, which nearly carpeted the ground. Jab wondered how many were cut from the trees that were here only a few months ago.

As Jab knelt in front of another writhing soldier, the screams from the hill intensified. Jab couldn't watch. Instead, he placed a paw on the soldier's face, careful not to touch his whiskers or snout. "Are you awake?"

"D-did the king do it?"

"What?"

"Did he d-defeat Nasalid's dogs?"

Jab wasn't about to tell a wounded soldier that he didn't like that "dogs" term, so instead he removed his helmet, avoiding the side of his chest with the lodged arrow. "He's still fighting."

"Of course he is." A weak, crooked smile spread across the wounded soldier's snout. "There's a reason they call him Steelfur. What's happening?"

Cheers erupted from the hill, and one word came out clearly. "Ridgerd! Ridgerd! Ridgerd!"

Nasalid's archers had scattered and scampered off, and Ridgerd was descending the hill.

At least one-fifth of the soldiers who had charged up with him had never joined and were scattered about the ground.

Another costly victory.

"He won," was all Jab could say.

The soldier laughed, though it came out more like a cough, and then his breathing slowed.

Jab's eyes watered.

The Droughtlands were supposedly an eternal desert bereft of water, but Jab wondered if this lake was that very place.

27

SANU

"Sheltercakes! Treat your family for a great price!"

"Pistachios by the satchel! Healthy foods for growing families!"

"Your kids won't eat if they're mad at you! Discount toys sold here!"

"Is a relative nagging you about not praying enough? Buy a prayer rock and prove your devotion!"

- Overheard chatter in ZelZaytun's market sector

On the way to the city's center, Sanu and Dilaal passed several frantic soldiers, each of which Dilaal calmed, pointing to Sanu and saying, "He returned. Back to your post."

Each time screwed more guilt into Sanu. "Thank you. I didn't think anyone would notice me leaving."

Dilaal cracked a smile. "You should have a higher opinion of yourself. Nasalid spoke highly of you and your brother to the point where I worry that my nephew back in Damouscus will get jealous."

Something about Nasalid having a family on another island struck a chord in Sanu. Nasalid was out here fighting for the holy island for all Grovekeepers everywhere, not just the locals. And yet it was locals like him and Jab who lost the most.

Merchants shouted out their wares and rodents of every variety crowded through the streets. Dilaal led them to a prayer hall, much smaller than the bigger one closer to the Gnaverwood's grove. Sanu glanced at the sky—it wasn't anywhere near the praying time. The only time Sanu had ever gone inside a prayer hall outside of praying with his family was to find Jab when Mom or Dad wanted him back home.

They walked inside and dusted off their tails, but Dilaal didn't direct him to the prayer space. Sanu peeked inside and noticed a family of squirrels praying together. A year ago, extra prayers with his family would've bored him to tears, but now, he hoped the kids in that family knew how good they had it.

Dilaal led them through a corridor past the washing area and down a flight of stairs. He opened an oak door, which revealed a seed cellar.

Nuts and seeds sat in sealed glass jars on long shelves over corked barrels.

Windows near the ceiling allowed scant light inside, and Sanu instantly tensed up. "Where are we?"

A hooded gerbil stepped out of the shadows. "You're late, Dilaal."

Dilaal placed a paw over his chest in mock apology. "There's plenty to snack on here if you're bored. I found the missing boy."

"The food is for the unhoused," the gerbil hissed. Removing his hood, he addressed Sanu, looking cleaner than the environment suggested. "This is where Nasalid's advisers meet in secret. Why his *brother* decided to bring you is beyond me."

Dilaal smiled angrily. "It's such a treat to only be known as someone's brother, even though I've overseen the successful acceptance of all the towns Nasalid's army emptied to frustrate the invaders. But I digress. Sanu here has information you all need to hear."

All?

Sanu glanced around the dark room, and other hooded rodents came forward, five in all.

They didn't all look Qawari, but he couldn't be sure.

"Um, yes," Sanu said. "Rattarossa won't listen to the Sapling, but I think Ridgerd will. Rattarossa is heading toward the lake depot."

"What?" the gerbil asked. "Ridgerd was going toward the lake."

"They both are," Dilaal said.

A jird came forward, speaking in the same accent as Nasalid and Dilaal. "Good. When they are all in one spot, they'll be easier to deal with."

A red squirrel shook his head, and the twigs in his beard clicked together. "No. We want them separated."

Sanu raised his paw. "They don't get along. If you can separate the two kings, you can negotiate with Ridgerd. He will listen to reason."

"This young man knows the Frenglese king well," Dilaal said. "They spent time together on Coppergrass."

"Nasalid was clear," the red squirrel replied. "We do not negotiate with the invaders. If they're willing to murder prisoners of war, they cannot be trusted."

"Well Nasalid isn't here, is he?" Dilaal asked the room. "His strategy of 'bury them in arrows' is only so effective against their armor. There's no more wood to make more arrows."

"You're forgetting the warships," the other jird offered. "With Kraksnout under our control, the warships protecting the island will cut off the invaders from their supply lines. We just have to wait them out."

Sanu clenched his fist. "Rodents will starve to death. Meet with Ridgerd."

The gerbil scratched his chin. "I think the boy has given us our solution. The kings are in conflict. Push them against each other, and they will do our job for us."

"Sending an envoy to one and not the other will do that," Dilaal said. "Besides, the Sapling is determined to reach out to the Freng king. If we do not impede her, we can act without disobeying Nasalid, since you care more about his opinion than mine."

Each of the five secret council members tapped their tails against the floor.

"I'll see you all soon," Dilaal said. "Stagger your exits."

Dilaal nudged Sanu to exit and head up the steps. "Since you know Steelfur so well, how can I get him to meet with me? How can I word things so he'll know I'm honest and don't want to kill him?"

"What do you mean?" Sanu asked, reaching the top step. "Nasalid promised he wouldn't kill him and nobody believed it."

Dilaal sighed and tapped his knuckle against the wall. "Exactly. He sounded too sincere. These nobles who play at politics all day are always expecting a trap, so you have to cater to that."

Sanu pondered the challenge as they passed the main prayer space. The squirrel family was still there. "Tell him I'm with you and I want a rematch in double siege."

Dilaal chuckled. "I'd hesitate to call a man who is my enemy a rodent of refined taste, but that's my favorite game."

Sanu could betray the man who'd saved his life or betray his island. He knew Ridgerd's military style matched his double siege strategy. "Tell him I'll translate for your meeting."

28

JAB

An unbelieving astronomer challenged Ganan, asking how He could preach about the All-Planter, who no rodent has ever seen or smelled. Ganan replied, "A mother had two daughters. The younger of the two refused her mother at every turn and was a constant source of heartache. The older served her mother and sister dutifully and was a joy. We know the mother loved them equally. We know that all children will gain a better appreciation for their parents as they age. Do you agree?" "Certainly," the astronomer replied. "But how? Love cannot be measured. And yet it is there, as is truth, as is beauty. Your science is useful, but it cannot glimpse the world inside our hearts. It also cannot identify the All-Planter."

- Excerpt from the Ganandeeds, "The Astronomer"

In the king's tent, Jab and Yagub huddled together over Ridgerd's map as Brouglas entered. The royal hamster paced, head stooped low.

Nodding to the hamster, the beaver said, "My king, we lost over one hundred soldiers taking that hill."

King Ridgerd grimaced. "I hate hills. I'll make them illegal back home. Twice now, I've won a battle that has felt like a loss."

Yagub pointed at the map. "If the scouts' report is true and Nasalid's main force is attacking Castle Kraksnout again, that means you have a chance to march into the Holy City. You won't have the same resistance."

"If you come over the hill, we can show you where the wall is weak from Nasalid's siege," Brouglas said.

Jab's heart raced. This was not how this meeting was supposed to go. "You could take it," Jab warned, "but you couldn't hold it. And while you're stuck there, Rattarossa could abandon the war and go straight to Freng and unite your brother and the other kings against you."

The hamster eyed Jab, eyebrow arched. "We don't know how Rattarossa has fared. He should've been here by now."

"Let's go to the top of the hill," Yagub said. "We'll show you how easily you can conquer it."

Ridgerd sighed. "I heard Grovekeepers on Qawar would wear headwraps to avoid looking at the Gnaverwood while Lady Marjitay and her father were in charge of the city. Is that true, Jab?"

Jab nodded. "Not all of us did, but I wore mine every day. I tried to avoid seeing the tree until Nasalid liberated the city."

The king rose from his seat, careful not to stand to his full height and bump his head into the tent's ceiling. "I will do the same. I won't gaze upon the city. I won't take what I can't hold, and I won't look at what I can't take."

"So you'll send everyone home then?" Jab asked.

Yagub scoffed.

"No," Ridgerd said. "There's a port nearby. We'll take that smaller town, then send ships to request troops from the Freng Islands, Coppergrass, and Rotteland. I'll keep a detachment here to hold the depot and await Rattarossa's arrival. Sir Brouglas, you'll remain here."

As he spoke, an exhausted porcupine opened the tent flap. "Forgive me, my king, but an emissary has arrived from Olihort. He says he speaks for Nasalid's brother, who is managing the city in his absence."

Jab bit back his anger at the Sprouter's name for the city, telling himself that anyone from Freng or Rotteland would've learned to say it as Olihort and not its true name. He needed to let go of his animosity toward the name, he knew, but it didn't make it sound any less grating to his ears.

Ridgerd straightened, getting the top of his head stuck in the tent. "You mean to tell me that Nasalid is willing to have a summit with me?"

"I could only imagine so," the messenger said. "It's his brother who asked to meet, after all."

Sanu must have succeeded, right as Jab failed to get Ridgerd off the island. Excitement over Sanu's victory erased Jab's disappointment over his own defeat.

"How do we know it's not a trap?" Yagub asked.

"Show His Majesty the letter," Sir Brouglas offered.

The messenger bowed and unrolled the parchment against his hip and pawed it to the king. Ridgerd skimmed it and smiled, then winked at Jab. "Your brother is well. I think he got in that old jird's ear. I would've liked to meet Nasalid himself, but his brother will do as a substitute."

Jab wondered how many rodents had said that about him, if Ridgerd and Brouglas would've preferred Sanu's company.

Within an hour, Ridgerd and a cohort of knights and archers took off toward the designated meeting spot, a team of scouts went southwest to scope out the port city, and the rest remained behind.

At Ridgerd's absence, a gloom fell over the camp, as if the king brought most of the energy with him. Jab wondered how many of the soldiers no longer felt invincible without Ridgerd Steelfur to lead them. If Nasalid's forces attacked again, even at reduced strength, they'd overpower the force here. A dark part of Jab wondered if Nasalid's lieutenants would bother to take prisoners in retribution for what happened at Kraksnout.

Jab paced along the lake's edge, hoping the waters would cleanse his foul memories of the place. Though the fishing boats that should've been there were gone, the pier stretching several dozen yards into the lake remained to suggest there had once been a supply depot here. He ventured down the dock, letting himself focus on the creaking wood, which was almost enough to silence the screams in his head. A third of the way into the lake, he felt distant from the hill that was now the resting place of dozens of Sprouters and Grovekeepers, the hill Ridgerd refused to summit all the way, lest he see the Holy City.

The pier extended far enough for Jab to spot ZelZaytun's walls, which looked like barely a fence around the holy Gnaverwood. And Jab noticed something that made his heart pound.

Rattarossa and his troops had arrived at the lake depot, and Ridgerd was gone.

Jab turned around to leave the empty dock and head back to the camp to tell Sir Brouglas, but a large rodent stood in his way.

It was King Rattarossa, holding an axe. "I've broken kings with gold. I only need iron for you."

Jab stiffened. "King Ridgerd will be back soon. You have to wait for him."

"First, your rat of a brother runs away, tells our secrets to Nasalid, and then he tries to turn my troops against me with words from the Sapling."

Rattarossa was big, and close enough that Jab couldn't see around him to the other side of the pier. He'd have to dive into the lake to get away, but he wasn't much of a swimmer, and Rattarossa's axe could take him out mid-jump.

"I'll kill you for what your brother did," Rattarossa said. "Unless you tell me what Nasalid is planning."

"I don't know," Jab said, backing up until his heel went over the pier's edge. "I've been with Ridgerd the whole time. I'm just a kid." Lies had saved his life before, but honesty would today. "A *real* king wouldn't kill a kid."

"Perhaps." Rattarossa closed the distance between them, swinging his axe. "But I'm an emperor. I do what I want."

29

SANU

I'm so sorry you had to watch Whima get killed by those brutes. I can't believe I put you in harm's way. Please forgive me, Sanu.

- A note from Cladh

Sanu and Dilaal, with a pawful of guards, hurried out of the city, passing through the healing district.

An outdoor barracks had been converted into an infirmary, where wounded soldiers with cuts from swords and puncture wounds from devil-beaks and crossbows moaned. Regular citizens of ZelZaytun tended to them. Dilaal didn't let them stop, but Sanu caught whispers. These soldiers had engaged Ridgerd's forces.

Snips of conversations all suggested the same thing. These wounded warriors had scurried from battle against Ridgerd and they all believed they would've triumphed if he hadn't been there. Sanu remembered the battles on Coppergrass, so he believed every word he heard, except the one about Ridgerd not needing to wear armor. There was no way his fur was actually made of steel.

Probably.

Once Sanu, Dilaal, and the guards left the gatehouse and mounted horses readied for them, Dilaal shook his head. "They won't go back to fight Ridgerd Steelfur. Half of Nasalid's force besieging Kraksnout are rodents who refused to fight him a second time. I imagine any of those we just saw who recover will join them too."

The chief guard, a grizzled gerbil with muscles barely contained by his armor, helped Sanu onto a horse. "The Kraksnout force won't be too happy if they win. Your brother will order them not to loot. Lots of the soldiers fighting for him now are already upset they couldn't loot ZelZaytun."

"Nasalid is following the warfare guidelines in the Divine Poetics," Sanu retorted, wishing Jab could hear him. "He's acting rightly." Sanu wished Jab would've been here to witness that; he would've been proud.

Dilaal led the group on the southwest road. "Nasalid is better liked by commoners than his own troops. Or at least, the troops who make noise. I'm sure the majority still are loyal to him. The bigger problem is the diminishing resources. *I'm* not even happy with him. Look at these bald lands. This was a lush forest when I came here a few months ago."

Dilaal gestured toward the hills south of the city. Sanu's tail curled tight. There *had* been lots of trees there. If the soldiers were low on morale and the resources were running out, Nasalid's greater numbers might not matter at all. ZelZaytun was in bigger danger than Sanu realized.

But after an hour of traveling, the blank landscape did make it easier to spot another group coming down the road.

This one had banners.

And lots of soldiers.

Dozens, maybe even hundreds more than was standard to meet a messenger. Sanu's heart raced. Ridgerd might have expected a double-cross and brought a force with him to fight or capture the messengers. But he had to know Sanu was with them, right? He wouldn't hurt him, not after what they'd been through on Coppergrass.

Dilaal's knuckles whitened as he clenched the reins. "Are those the banners of Ridgerd Steelfur?"

Sanu didn't need to see the colors of the banner or the symbols, because they were close enough to see one rodent above all the rest.

There were certainly other rodents in the Great Sea who were as tall as King Ridgerd, but it wasn't just the size. Even from a distance, Sanu noticed how he carried himself.

"It's him," was all Sanu could say.

"This might be more than the discussion over a double siege match that I was expecting," Dilaal said.

"He's a Freng dog," the chief guard said. "What else do you expect?"

"Not all Frenglese are like that," Sanu snapped. Ridgerd, Cladh, and Brouglas were all good rodents. Honorable. Better rodents than most Qawari Sanu knew.

Dilaal called for a halt, and Ridgerd's force came the rest of the way.

Once they were all within speaking distance, a trumpeter blew a triple-note, and began announcing. "You stand before King—"

"Sanu!" the royal hamster exclaimed, bounding over. "You're safe!"

The trumpeter grumbled and placed his trumpet at his side.

Ridgerd wrapped Sanu in a hug, then pointed at him, announcing to his troops. "This lad saved my life back on Coppergrass. He will make a fine translator for our summit. Very trustworthy."

Dilaal urged his horse forward and spoke in flawless Frenglese. "I am Dilaal, brother to Nasalid the Liberator and caretaker of ZelZaytun. Sanu will assist in translation if needed, but I am versed in your tongue. Since you have brought quite the force with you, Ridgerd, you must excuse what little I have to offer them."

Two bodyguards slid off their saddles and began assembling a tent.

"I have enough food and refreshment for you and a translator if you would like one, but that is all. Sanu has told me you enjoy double siege. I was hoping we could play while we discuss."

Ridgerd addressed his troops. "Take a seat, lads! They come in peace." Ridgerd's rodents broke formation and either sat in the grass or leaned against their horses.

Dilaal opened the tent flap and motioned for the hamster to enter first. "Stories of your size have not been exaggerated. I ordered a taller tent to accommodate you better."

Ridgerd arched an eyebrow and glanced at Sanu. "Was this your idea? Did seeing me bump my head in that ship every day inspire you?"

Sanu smiled. "No, sir. I would've said to lower it."

"Ha! I'd tousle your hair for that if I weren't wearing armor."

Inside the tent, the two guards had set up a double siege board on a table with two chairs. Sanu took up a post against the tent wall, and a soldier he didn't recognize stood against the opposite wall, eyeing the chief bodyguard.

"Did Sanu tell you my strategy?" Ridgerd asked.

"He wouldn't breathe a word of it," Dilaal replied. They took a minute politely quibbling over who should go first.

Sanu clenched his fist. "Rodents are dying."

Both leaders gaped at him.

"You heard me," Sanu insisted. "Dilaal, Ridgerd wants you to go second so he can trick you into thinking you have the upper paw. Ridgerd, Dilaal wants to see how you play because he thinks that will give him insight into how you think and then he can manipulate you. Skip the game and stop this stupid war."

Sanu expected Ridgerd's whiskers to stiffen like when he was angry, but they drooped instead. "Fine. Dilaal, turn ZelZaytun over to the Sprouters. It is an object of worship for us. Consider that me moving my general piece out first." He knocked on the table, a habit of ending a game turn that Sanu had seen on Coppergrass.

"An object of worship?" Dilaal shook his head at the king. "It is for us too. My brother's terms were generous, and you spurned them. You must turn back if you wish to keep your life and let your soldiers return to their families."

Sanu marched to the double siege table and snatched the red general piece. "Ridgerd, be honest with Dilaal. You think you'll go to the Droughtlands when you die for some reason you refuse to tell me."

Ridgerd sighed. "You've changed, Sanu. 'Tis true, Dilaal. My soldiers believe conquering the Holy City will allow them passage into the Walled Garden."

Dilaal grabbed the blue general piece and offered it to Ridgerd. "Funny. My brother believed the same thing a year ago. He'd committed such violence under our uncle's leadership that he believed uniting Grovekeepers to retake ZelZaytun would be his only way out of the Droughtlands. You seem like a good rodent, King Ridgerd. Would you kill me for my faith?"

After some slow blinks, Ridgerd shook his head. "Of course not."

"What about me, Ridgerd?" Sanu asked.

"Why are you asking me something like that, Sanu? You were like a younger brother to me back on Coppergrass."

Sanu placed the red general piece in Ridgerd's paw beside the blue one. "You would do what Nasalid did. Claim the war is over, and let everyone live in peace. Isn't that your goal?"

"Yes, but—"

"Listen to the boy." Dilaal raised a paw. "You have no need to be here. Go home and end the bloodshed."

"That's where you're wrong," Ridgerd said. "As much as I wish to stop, Rattarossa will not. You would much prefer my banners flying over ZelZaytun than his. It was nice to meet you, Dilaal. And Sanu, I am happy to see you're well." Ridgerd placed the two general pieces gently in the double siege box. "But this negotiation will get us nowhere. Goodbye."

As he stood, Sanu rushed to grab his wrist. "The Sapling in ZelZaytun will cleanse you of your sins. I know you all have rituals for that."

"All the rituals in the world won't change my father's last words or what will happen if I return to my kingdom empty-pawed. I'm sorry, Sanu. Jab is still at my camp. I will tell him you're well."

Dilaal slumped in his chair and buried his face in his paws.

The tent flap closed.

Hearing that Jab was well lifted Sanu's spirits for only half a second. The council members had said that Rattarossa's battalion was moving south to meet up with Ridgerd's main force. That meant Jab would be with Rattarossa without the king to help him.

Jab was in danger.

30

JAB

One day, I hope to make it to Qawar. Nothing would fill me with more gladness than to visit some of the places you did.

— *From the prayer journal of Sir Brouglas*

"Danger" was an understatement.

Jab had returned to this lake many times in his nightmares, so it seemed fitting that he'd die by the paw of a monster on this stupid pier.

Emperor Rattarossa swung his axe, and Jab ducked, losing some hair off his ear in the process, and getting a glimpse of two Barkheart Order knights guarding the other end of the pier. Wood splintered where Rattarossa's axe had connected with the pier.

"Help!" Jab shouted. "Help!"

"Nobody's coming." Rattarossa prepared for another swing. Jab had maneuvered a little to the left to avoid the swing, but that just put him in more of a corner.

The dormouse swung, and Jab dove between Rattarossa's legs, pulling his tail. Metal thuds sounded in the distance, shaking the wooden planks underneath them.

Rattarossa whipped his ship mast of a tail, jiggling Jab off. "You want to run off to Nasalid too?"

Jab sidestepped an overhead swing.

"Stand still," Rattarossa said, before adding something in Rottelander.

Jab came at him from the side and coiled his tail around the dormouse's armored ankle, but he was too heavy to trip and he ended up cutting his tail.

Rattarossa kneed Jab in the stomach, sending him to the wood, skidding until his ears hung over the pier's edge and his hindpaw caught in the broken planks.

Gasping for air, Jab stared up at the sky, unwilling to look the monster in the eye. The sky was darkened from the Gnaverwood's shadow.

While most rodents would fear the darkness, it was a calming sight for Jab. He'd spent so much of his life trying to avoid looking at the tree, that it was a comforting final image. He hoped he'd make it to the Walled Garden on Pruning Day, where he'd be reunited with his parents and Sanu.

Thuds shook the dock's wooden planks; the final axe swing didn't come.

Steel on steel clanged, and Jab snapped his attention toward his attacker. A longsword blocked Rattarossa's axe.

Sir Brouglas had fought through the Barkheart Order knights and had come to Jab's rescue.

"What kind of rodent kills a child?" Brouglas hissed. "Run, lad."

Jab scrambled to his hindpaws, scurrying behind the beaver. The two fighters' weapons remained locked as they struggled to gain the footing to earn the upper paw. Rattarossa boasted several inches and several pounds over Brouglas, and the beaver's knees buckled.

Jab wasn't about to let Brouglas die. He ran over to the splintered plank from Rattarossa's earlier attack and pried it off, creating a club for himself.

The two warriors had broken off, and Brouglas panted like he'd been running all day. Dents in his armor and trickles of blood dripping from the joints suggested those Barkhearts hadn't been pushovers.

"I said run, Jab!"

Rattarossa swung at Brouglas, who countered with his kite shield.

Jab couldn't do much with a club, but he didn't have much else since his crossbow was back ashore. He charged at the brute, hoping to hit his knee hard enough to knock him off his hindpaws.

"No." Brouglas spun, tripping Jab with his paddle tail.

As Jab fell, Rattarossa's axe came down, slicing off the beaver's wrist.

Brouglas screamed and sank to his knees as his dropped sword clanged against the pier.

He'd put himself in a vulnerable position to save Jab.

"Weakling," Rattarossa muttered. He lifted his axe, catching a glint of sunlight in the metal, casting a different shadow over Jab. His last protector was defeated.

Jab scrambled to get Brouglas's dropped sword, even though he had no clue how to use it.

As he did, the planks rattled again.

Brouglas had gotten back up and tackled Rattarossa, sending them both over the edge.

The splash drenched Jab, washing the blood off the sword.

Both warriors were in heavy metal armor.

Jab peered over the side, trying to figure out which vortex of bubbles belonged to Brouglas. He wanted to dive in, but they'd disappeared under the murky water.

The bubbles stopped.

His heart dropped to his stomach and tears flowed. Brouglas had drowned, taking Rattarossa with him.

More thuds shook the planks underneath him, but Jab didn't care who they belonged to. This ridiculous war would not stop claiming lives. But for Brouglas to die? Jab hated how pointless it all was. The beaver knight had known he'd drown in his suit of armor. Brouglas was there when an armored soldier fell overboard on their way to Coppergrass. He knew exactly what would happen and did it anyway.

For Jab, a worthless liar and a failure.

His vision blurred as he gazed upon the water, the final resting place of Sir Brouglas the beaver knight. Brouglas didn't think Jab was worthless. He gave his life to prove it. Without fighting the flowing tears, Jab made himself a new promise. Brouglas had given Jab a chance at a new life.

He'd take it.

Jab collected himself and stood, brushing a tear away with his tail, since his paws now held all that was left of Brouglas, except his journal and his copy of the *Ganandeeds*.

Yagub stormed up the pier with a Barkheart knight at his side.

"What happened?" Yagub asked. "Where's Brouglas?"

The words wouldn't come out. Jab pointed at the lake with his tail and displayed the beaver's weapons.

"And the emperor?" the Barkheart asked in a thick Rottelander accent.

Those words *could* come out. Jab glared at him. "He tried to kill me. Brouglas saved me. They're both at the bottom now."

"What?" Yagub gasped and ran a paw through his hair. "That's impossible." His voice cracked. "He-he was like a father to me."

The knight removed his helmet, revealing himself to be a dormouse. Jab wasn't sure what he'd expected, but seeing a regular rodent underneath that armor felt odd. "We can't let that be the story." He lifted his eyes to the sky and muttered something in Rottelander. Jab did catch "Ganan" in whatever he said. Changing back to Frenglese, the knight continued, "Emperor Rattarossa jumped into the lake."

The noise Yagub made was somewhere between a scoff and whimper. "What? Brouglas tackled him to save Jab's life. We saw the tail end of it."

"No," the knight said. "The emperor was so overjoyed at the sight of the holy tree and the beautiful serenity of this lake that he felt compelled to jump in the lake without thought to his armor. He wanted to boost morale so much that he ignored his safety."

"That's what you're going to tell everyone?" Jab asked, wiping the last tear from his eye.

The knight's eyes looked shallow. "Would you prefer the troops to hear that one of Ridgerd's soldiers killed him? How do you think that will go over?"

"So nobody will get to know what Brouglas did for me?" Jab gripped the sword's hilt and the shield's handle. They were both heavy for him, but he'd get used to the weight.

"He saved you from drowning yourself? We could say that," Yagub offered. "At least he'll be remembered as a hero."

"Do you think they're going to believe it?" Jab asked.

The knight put his helmet back on. "I think they'll prefer to hear it that way. Our emperor coveted the Frenglese islands, but I think his soldiers would be wary of going to war without him. We won't start a war over one rodent's memory. But hearing it another way..."

"So what's next?" Jab asked.

"The responsibility of liberating Olihort falls solely on King Ridgerd's shoulders," the knight said. "We'll see if he's up to the task."

Jab glanced over his shoulder at the lake. The hairs Jab had lost in the fight had already blown away, and the broken planks were all that showed a sign of a struggle. The lake was calm again, having swallowed Jab and Sanu's savior.

31

SANU

"When we were boys, Nasalid only had dreams of becoming a prayer warden and scholar. I wanted to be a fighter. But all the rodents in Gerdiz feared that the Sprouters would expand to our island, being so close to Qawar. Our uncle made us both fight. What can I say? He was the better soldier. He had to drop his pursuits, but he never neglected his prayers."

- Dilaal's response to a question about his childhood

Sanu shielded his eyes against the wrathful sun, wishing the Gnaverwood's shadow covered this part of the island right now. After some debate with his guards, Dilaal insisted they go directly to ZelZaytun instead of sending someone north to inform Nasalid about their summit. "He gave us the answer to defeating him," Dilaal said on their approach to the city's walls. "And Sanu's stories confirm it."

Sanu's heart thumped faster. "What do you mean?"

"It's his guilt," Dilaal said with a grin. "He's no different from Nasalid in that regard. His sense of honor born from his faith is his weakness."

The gates to ZelZaytun rose with a *racka-click* and they entered the barracks which had become an open-air hospital.

"A sense of honor isn't a weakness," Sanu hissed.

Dilaal glanced over his shoulder at him. "Are you sure? Do you know how many troops grumble about my brother because he won't let them loot and pillage from the Sprouters? Do you know how much faster this conflict would've ended if he'd refused to let his commanders call for retreats?"

Sanu almost fell off his horse. While his feelings about Nasalid had become more complicated over the last few months, his insistence on trying to fight a just war had been the one thing convincing Sanu that he was a Liberator and not a tyrant. "Those are good things though," Sanu insisted.

One of the guards shrugged. "Tell that to them." He gestured toward the wounded soldiers lying in rows of cots whose collective moans forced them to speak louder to hear each other.

The other guard nodded. "Nasalid had a chance to destroy all the Barkhearts and set fire to their monastery last month. He refused to attack what he called 'holy rodents' in peacetime."

"So, what are you going to do?" Sanu asked.

"It's simple, really," Dilaal replied, leading them toward the city center. "I'll starve him out. These soldiers are too tired and hurt to confront him, and Nasalid hasn't returned with his force from Kraksnout yet. The troops we do have, though, can pinch his force from east and west, slowly forcing them into the lake. Too far north, and they are within range of our archers on the walls. Too far south, and they go into another abandoned port town. It appears to be a plain fact that Ridgerd can't be felled in battle, but if he's forced to watch his soldiers starve, his sense of honor will compel him to surrender or put himself into enough of a risky situation that we can capture him."

Sanu's mouth dried. "I see." He remembered King Ridgerd saving Sanu's life on Coppergrass twice and risking his life for disloyal soldiers who hated him. "But you said these troops are too weak to fight."

"They are," Dilaal replied flippantly. "But not the reinforcements who were going to relieve Nasalid later today. They can go south instead."

Dilaal would endanger Nasalid, and use the low morale against him. This was underpawed betrayal. It made a twisted kind of sense, monstrous as it was.

Reaching the city center, staring at the Gnaverwood with the grand Gananhall beside it, inspired an idea.

"Dilaal, I'm going to see the Sapling."

Dilaal narrowed his eyes. "The last time you did, you ran away and sent the city into a panic."

With a half-chuckle, Sanu looked down at the street and scratched the back of his head. "She invited me. And I thought she'd want to know what Ridgerd said."

Dilaal waved his paw. "Fine. I don't need you tagging along anyway. Nasalid got enough criticism for letting your brother sit in on so many important planning sessions and I won't be accused of the same."

Sanu turned, but a guard whistled, making him freeze.

"Leave my horse. You're a flight risk."

"Ah, yes, sorry." Sanu halted and dismounted, pawing the reins back to the guard.

Sanu shuddered, realizing the last time he'd been in the Sapling's office, it had belonged to someone else. The previous ruler of ZelZaytun had murdered the former Sapling in cold blood, and Jab had come dangerously close to killing Sanu over a case of mistaken identity. Cladh's warm presence didn't do much to ease the pain of the memory.

While Cladh's acorn amulet wasn't a new sight, seeing it on her in here made it almost impossible to focus.

"Thanks for telling me about Dilaal. I can't believe he'd undermine Nasalid like that," Cladh said.

Sanu curled his tail, trying to refocus. He was glad he'd told her the story on the way up the stairs instead of here. "I think Nasalid needs to know. Can I borrow Vermitch again?"

Cladh arched an eyebrow. "Do you have any idea what kind of Droughtlands I caught after your last trip out of the city?"

"I'll wear a disguise." Revisiting Jab's semi-accidental attempt on Sanu's life a few months ago did have one benefit. That day, Jab had used a baker's cinnamon to change the color of his fur for a few hours.

"Now we're talking," Cladh said. She rose from her desk and opened a gold-trimmed cedar cabinet. Inside was a row of vestments and robes that looked too fancy to be worn, more like tapestries than clothes. "How would you like to be a seedling? I'd give you some of my Sapling gear, but I don't think anyone would believe you're me."

Sanu let out an awkward chuckle. "Because I'm so big and strong and manly, right?"

Cladh snorted a laugh and Sanu tried to keep the hurt from showing on his face. "You're a squirrel. Your tail looks nothing like my little nub." After clearing her throat, Cladh added, "Give yourself a break. You're young." She reached between silken garments and pulled out a plain white robe with a hood. "Seedling Sanu."

Sanu accepted the robe and fumbled with it. *Young?* He'd show her.

"That part goes over your head," Cladh instructed. "Your arm isn't coming out because that's the hood."

After an awkward minute of struggle, Sanu got his arms, legs, and tail out of the right spots and pulled the hood over his head. "Convincing?"

"Not really," Cladh said. "Nasalid let a lot of Lady Marjitay's former guards keep their jobs, which means you can expect some Sprouters at all the gates." She knelt and grabbed a box from the floor of the cabinet about the size of a double siege set. It made Sanu almost regret interrupting Ridgerd and Dilaal's match. She opened the box and pulled out a necklace in the same style as her amulet, but this was a walnut, split in half and coated in bronze. "Put this on."

Sanu accepted the offering and wore it like a necklace. "What's this for?"

"It's a sign that you're fasting. The gatekeepers who see it will recognize it as a sign that you won't be talking."

Sanu's ear twitched. He forgot that other groups fasted and felt a little unintelligent. "You fast from talking? Do you eat normally?"

"Minimal talking, eating, and drinking," Cladh replied. "Any Sprouter who sees you in this getup won't ask you too many questions."

Sanu nodded and checked himself in her mirror, which was framed in gold. He didn't look like himself and wondered what Jab would say if he saw him. Jab had thought it was bad enough to pretend to be a Sprouter, so Sanu couldn't imagine his reaction at impersonating a seedling.

"But what will I say if someone stops me?" Sanu asked. "I can't tell them I'm going to Nasalid."

"Why not?" Cladh asked. "Your Sapling commands it and you're oath-bound to obey. Come on, let's get Vermitch ready."

Sanu followed her, gaining a new appreciation for why King Ridgerd had such mixed opinions about the religious hierarchy. Not that Sanu minded listening to Cladh.

32

JAB

A mystic who had traveled to Qawar from Kinoumi begged to exchange wisdom with Ganan, for news of Him had traveled far. The mystic followed the Brightness and believed rodents were reborn, and asked Ganan what He thought about what happened after we die. Ganan's followers assumed they would argue, but they sipped tea and joked. They parted ways and thanked each other. "What did you say to him? We expected a heated debate," a follower demanded. "I spoke to him of the Walled Garden and the Droughtlands, as he requested, and he told me that in the Brightness, leading a good life leads to a better one after this and choosing cruelty leads to a more difficult one. What's there to debate? We spent the rest of the time discussing flower arrangement."

- Excerpt from the Ganandeeds,
  "The Kinoumi Mystic"

Clutching Brouglas's sword and shield, Jab staggered off the docks with Yagub and the Barkheart knight, where soldiers with Ridgerd's symbols crowded in on the left and Rattarossa's troops pressed in on the right, with other Barkhearts staggered among them.

"Foul and tragic news," the knight said. He said something else in Rottelander, and Jab assumed he was repeating himself. "Our Emperor Rattarossa has drowned in the lake."

Gasps and dropped jaws ran through the crowd. More than a few soldiers cried out to Ganan. Others cast suspicious eyes at Jab.

"Yagub, tell them about Brouglas," Jab whispered.

"Not yet," Yagub said. "I liked him better, but Rattarossa is more important."

The Barkheart continued the "jumping in the lake" story in Rottelander, and angry shouts answered in both languages.

"We're not paying for his funeral!"

"Where's our money?"

"He promised us titles and land. What happens to that?"

The Barkheart shouted back, but Ridgerd's soldiers joined in.

"Fight with us!"

"Ridgerd will treat you well!"

One of Rattarossa's soldiers threw his helmet onto the ground and spat. Then he walked away.

"Where are you going?" the Barkheart demanded. "Are you deserting?"

The individual, a sour-looking lemming, unsheathed his sword. "I know Rattarossa trusted you Barkhearts with his treasure. If you aren't going to pay us, I'm not fighting."

Three others from Rattarossa's forces did the same.

"You have nowhere to go!" the Barkheart shouted.

Jab wasn't about to miss an opportunity. He rushed in front of the Barkheart. "Nasalid is honorable. If you surrender your weapons, you'll get passage back home or he'll let you live on Qawar. That's what he promised after defeating Lady Marjitay. You don't even have to become a Grovekeeper."

This caused more murmurs.

Another Barkheart pointed at Jab. "Liar! Nasalid murdered all the Sprouters in Olihort."

Yagub joined Jab. "I was there when it happened, and so was my knight, Sir Brouglas, who also drowned in that lake. Nasalid did *not* kill a single rodent who wasn't fighting him. I don't love that there isn't a Sprouter on King Suleimouse's throne, but Nasalid is honorable. Did the truth come to Rotteland?"

The first lemming shoved his sword into the dirt and pointed at the Gnaverwood in the distance. "Olihort is that way, huh?"

"Call it ZelZaytun," Jab said, "but yes."

Another ten soldiers dropped their swords and axes and headed toward the Holy City with them, as did one of Ridgerd's soldiers and a pawful of camp followers from both sides. Jab couldn't believe his luck and thanked the All-Planter. Without the kings, the already-low morale was shaken.

"Stop them!" the Barkheart shouted. "Kill the deserters!"

The other Barkhearts in the crowd raised their weapons. Some of Rattarossa's troops made way for them, others drew their own swords and axes.

"Stop!"

Jab knew that voice.

King Ridgerd had returned to the cheers of his soldiers.

The deserters stopped in their tracks, as did the scuffles between the Barkhearts and Rattarossa's other troops.

"Someone tell me what's happened. Where is your king?"

"Rattarossa died, my liege," Yagub said. "Some of his men want to abandon the war."

Ridgerd dismounted from his horse, and a team of his followers attended to it. He pointed at the Barkheart on the dock with Jab and Yagub. "You are his second?"

"Yes, King Ridgerd," the dormouse replied.

"If your troops are deserting, take that as a sign of weak leadership."

The Barkheart gripped his devilbeak. "Some of yours left too."

Ridgerd turned to his force. "Anyone who wants to abandon the pilgrimage, be my guest. I will only have the willing by my side. What I ask is too dangerous for anyone to join with half a heart. If you doubt your strength and resolve now, I shudder to think what you'll do when surrounded by the enemy. Go now and I won't think less of you." He faced Rattarossa's soldiers.

"Any of you who are here as pilgrims may remain with me. Your late king had ambitions of empire. Any of you who are here as conquerors would do well to leave. With your king's passing, much will be in turmoil in Rotteland, and you'll have your homes to attend to. What happens if local barons get into power struggles? Let's take the night to weigh our options. Join me or depart in the morning."

The Barkheart marched toward Ridgerd. "You can't—"

He loomed over the armored dormouse. "I can. I did. I will again. I have little patience for holy leaders who force their ways onto others. If you want the Holy City in Sprouter paws again, your only way is with me."

The Barkheart backed off and huffed.

Jab nudged Yagub. "We have to tell Ridgerd the rest of what happened."

"You're right." Yagub sighed, staring at the ground. "I can't believe Brouglas is gone."

They left the dock and started toward Ridgerd. "You don't *still* want to be one of those Barkhearts, do you?" Jab asked.

"Not if they act like this," Yagub replied. "They're not living the values."

Once they reached the king, Ridgerd smiled at them. "Jab, I have much to tell you about my short trip."

"So do we," Jab said.

"Where's Sir Brouglas?" the king asked.

Yagub motioned toward the huge group of soldiers staring at them. "Can we talk in your tent?"

33

SANU

"Don't ask him for anything, he's fasting."

"He can still nod or shake his head or wave his tail. Seedling! If you see Rattarossa, tell him I'll see him in the Droughtlands!"

"Watch your mouth! That's a seedling."

— Gatehouse chatter as
Sanu left ZelZaytun

With the Holy City behind him, Sanu burst along the north road, sped by Vermitch. Sanu knew the steed was too young to have traveled all over the Great Sea with the beaver knight, but he liked imagining that Brouglas had been astride Vermitch at the Battle of Phranktonbourg, doing whatever heroic things there earned him distinction. But if nothing else, the beaver had ridden Vermitch when he did the most heroic thing possible for Sanu and saved his life at Rattin's horns.

It had only been a few months, but it felt like a lifetime. And then they'd been sent to Castle Kraksnout on a mission to empty the garrison and defend ZelZaytun against Nasalid. Remembering the garrison, Sanu realized there might have been some Barkheart knights. They had been so eager for battle and ready to kill Grovekeepers to keep the Holy City under Lady Marjitay's paw.

Hours in the saddle at full speed made Sanu's legs wobble. Vermitch would need a rest soon, and Sanu didn't have a spare horse or a ton of supplies beyond food and water for the pair of them. He'd only brought Dad's scimitar on his belt and a rolled-up tent strapped to the saddle. The craggy desert landscape would soon slope up into the more hilly territory where Castle Kraksnout loomed.

With sunset threatening, Sanu slowed Vermitch to a stop, and found a withered tree to tie him to. Sanu wondered how many wars this tree had witnessed. Giving it a light knock on its whitened bark made Sanu worry it would snap in half, but he didn't exactly have anything else to tie Vermitch to.

Petting the horse and offering him a carrot, Sanu checked for any cuts or signs of damage, worried he might have nicked him with his scimitar. He'd been riding Vermitch for so long that he wanted to make sure he hadn't hurt the brave animal. Sanu wondered if some part of Vermitch understood how urgent this message to Nasalid was, and how many lives were at stake, even the future of two religions. Ridgerd was the leader he respected more, but Nasalid was the one Qawar needed more.

The sun touched the horizon, and Sanu used a tiny bit of his water to wash his paws so he could pray. Knowing Jab was out there at this moment praying, and Nasalid was too, along with every Grovekeeper in the Great Sea, gave him a measure of comfort, despite being so alone. He wished Cladh had sent him someone else to accompany him, but after what happened to Whima, Sanu understood why. He attracted bad luck and bad decisions.

When Sanu finished praying, Vermitch huffed, clopping his hooves and kicking up dust. Sanu didn't even have a chance to light a campfire yet. In these sparse grasses and craggy hills, he couldn't imagine what could spook a horse, but Sanu placed one paw on his scimitar and the other on the horse's stomach, desperate to calm the steed.

That's when Sanu heard them.

The yips.

Hyenas.

In the fading light, Sanu noticed gleaming eyes, and he prayed that the moonlight wouldn't be blocked by the Gnaverwood. He knew hyenas hunted in packs, but he couldn't remember their pack size. He unsheathed his scimitar.

Nasalid needed that message. Qawar needed him to reach Nasalid.

Vermitch whinnied and struggled against the rope.

"Whoa," Sanu soothed.

With a yip and a snarl, a hyena lunged from the left. Sanu sidestepped, trying to slash in the same motion, but the beast clamped onto his tail. He thought he'd known pain when a crossbow bolt went through his ear, but this was on another level.

Sanu screamed, trying to flick the thing off, but it had latched onto him. He swung his scimitar, slicing into the monster's ribs. Yowling, the mass of spots and muscles fell.

His tail throbbed so painfully he almost blacked out. But he would keep fighting despite the blood trickling from his tail.

Vermitch backed up and kicked, hitting a second hyena and snapping his rope in the same motion.

"Vermitch!" Sanu called.

The horse squealed, and galloped into the darkness, carrying all Sanu's supplies with him except his scimitar, his waterskin, and his one log of firewood. Sanu was bleeding so much that he heard each heartbeat in his ears. A third hyena charged through the darkness, and lunged.

Breathing hard, Sanu dodged, and the hyena's teeth sank into Sanu's sleeve. Sanu thunked the beast in the head with the pommel of his sword, and it unlatched, giving him room to follow it up with a slice into its ribs, but he didn't cut as much as he had with the first.

Yip yip yip

Sanu sank to a knee, feeling lightheaded. The hyena which had attacked him first limped away, leaving a trail of staggered tracks.

The third hyena wheeled around and coiled for another lunge.

Sanu was ready for it this time. He held his scimitar lower and spun with it. He missed the beast's face, but he got its paws. It collapsed into the sparse grass.

Sanu limped over to where Vermitch had kicked the second hyena, and the animal wasn't moving.

Thank the All-Planter.

Sanu removed his shirt and shivered in the cold. He wrapped the clothes as tightly around his tail as possible to stop the bleeding. Once he felt the bleeding stop, he sipped the little water he had left. The hyenas weren't defeated, but that had at least bought him time. Two were out of commission, and one was limping away.

Still, Sanu didn't feel safe. He climbed the withered tree and laid down on the biggest branch. He'd once heard scholars claim that squirrels lived in trees in the ancient past, but it sounded ridiculous. But finding an almost-comfortable spot that didn't feel like it would snap off made him second-guess himself. As long as he came back to the road, he'd make it. Nasalid needed warriors, and the rodents of Qawar needed justice. That would have to be enough for him for now.

He just hoped he'd wake up.

34

JAB

I've taken an open position for a senior knight of the Goose Clan in Qawar. The rumor is that Lady Marjitay is such a tyrant that nobody wants to work for her, but this allows me a chance to become a life-long pilgrim in Qawar.

- From the prayer journal
of Sir Brouglas

Jab examined the rations placed in front of him. A tiny sliver of fish, yet it was the same size as Ridgerd's. The royal hamster didn't take a larger portion than anyone. Ridgerd had insisted they all say a prayer before eating while Jab prayed outside. Now that he was back, Jab realized they'd all waited for him to start eating.

Yagub seemed more patient with Jab now that Brouglas was gone, and that effect apparently spread to the two other commanders and seedling in the tent.

Sanu had often described Ridgerd's joviality to Jab, but it seemed to have evaporated.

"Gentlerodents," Ridgerd began, "it pains me to hear that Rattarossa tried to murder Jab. I wish I could have traded places with Sir Brouglas. Were it up to me, that cruel tyrant wouldn't even get a plaque near the lake to say he died there, and our dear beaver knight would get a procession to rival my father's."

"What kind of craven rodent attacks a child?" hissed one of the commanders.

"The most brutal rodents are also the weakest," the seedling mused.

Ridgerd gestured to Jab. "How are you? I know you've been close to death before, but I imagine you're rattled."

Jab wished he'd been stronger. Faster. Smarter. Anything-er. Sir Brouglas didn't deserve to die. He would've fought Rattarossa off if Jab hadn't tried to help. But this wasn't the time for that. "I... I miss him. He saved my life and my brother's. I can never repay him."

"That's the difficult thing with the dead." Ridgerd's gaze lifted to the tent's pointed ceiling. "There's no appeasing them."

Silence hung in the air until Yagub shifted in his seat. "What will you do about the Rottelander soldiers?"

The larger of the two commanders, a grizzled porcupine responded. "Flog the ones who attempted to desert. Then we build battering rams and take Olihort."

"With what wood?" the seedling asked. "Nasalid's peasants have stripped the land of its resources. I was honestly surprised we found any fish in the lake."

Jab stared down at his plate. It looked more like what a fish would eat than a meal fit for a rodent. Jab turned it over with his fork, wondering where his appetite had gone as his gaze drifted to Brouglas's sword and shield.

Ridgerd swallowed the last of his food. "Without siege equipment, we'll never break down the walls of the Holy City. Jab, Yagub, is there some hidden entrance into the city?"

There could've been, for all Jab knew. "No," Jab said. "There isn't. Nasalid wears chainmail to sleep. He's paranoid. If there were secret passages, he would've had them covered up."

Yagub shrugged. "Brouglas never showed me any. Unless you want to dig your way inside by going through the hill."

"And risk damaging the Gnaverwood's roots?" Ridgerd asked. "Never."

Ridgerd's faithfulness was on full display. Jab had spent so long thinking Sprouters were wicked, yet *he* had been the closed-minded one. Jab had always believed that the holy tree was invincible, but he didn't say it, because he knew what *wasn't* invincible. "If you charged a gate, how many soldiers would you lose?"

"Too many," Ridgerd said.

The older commander scowled at Jab, and the younger one, a lemming with immaculate hair, arched an eyebrow.

"We have to go home," the lemming said. "We can't take the Holy City without siege equipment and there is no wood here to make more."

"We can't go home," Ridgerd said. "I know you want to return to your family estate; trust me, I understand that feeling, but if we go home and promise to return with a better-equipped force, we'll never get our momentum back. We're so close to Olihort, I can taste it."

"So, let's get it," the seedling said.

Jab's arm hairs stood on end. "King Ridgerd, you said you won't capture what you can't defend. Even with the loyal soldiers in Rattarossa's army, it won't be enough to fight off Nasalid again. He has lots of islands under his control."

Ridgerd leaned toward the table. "We'll head south to the port city. If it's abandoned, we'll use the materials that are there to build siege engines. We'll also prepare a boat for any deserters."

The porcupine commander bristled at the suggestion, rattling his quills.

"I'll make you the captain of that ship if you keep huffing over there," Ridgerd said. "If the town isn't abandoned, we'll do the same. They will support our claim."

"The town south of here is my hometown of Banuj," Yagub said. "It's mostly Sprouters, so you should be well-received there."

Ridgerd sighed and made for the tent's exit. "I'll inform the men of what we're doing. We'll move out in the morning. Jab, come with me. Bring Sir Brouglas's sword and shield with you."

Thankful to be away from the almost-food, Jab hurried to follow the colossal king. Even though the last of the sun had set, fine pinks and oranges danced together in the western horizon. Jab looked for the moon, but couldn't find it. He hoped Sanu was out there on the other side of the Gnaverwood, kept safe by the moonlight. The hyenas would come prowling soon, if the old folks' stories were true.

"Jab, tell it to me plain. Did you provoke Rattarossa?"

"What? No." Jab almost laughed at the question, but then the confrontation replayed in his head. A glance at Sir Brouglas's equipment made the truth rise to the surface. "He said he wanted to kill Sanu and that he'd kill me first. I think he planned to do something to torture Sanu. I don't fully understand why. But I swear by ZelZaytun, I didn't provoke him. He cornered me."

"It's because your brother ran away from us, which Rattarossa saw as an embarrassment." Ridgerd sighed. "Getting in trouble for your brother's actions. I don't blame either of you though. He must have seemed like a monster to you. He certainly seemed like one to me."

He was real though, which made him worse than any imaginary beast. A shiver ran up Jab's spine from his tail to his neck.

"Are you worried about what your brother is doing now?" Jab asked. He needed to try. Ridgerd going to a port away from the Holy City was getting him closer to *leaving* the holy island. "Since you said you thought Rattarossa would make a deal with him to steal your throne."

Ridgerd walked back over to his tent and rang a bell. Soldiers slowly emerged from their own tents and left their campfires.

Before addressing the troops, Ridgerd turned to Jab. "Rattarossa's death has bought me some time. I haven't forgotten about my subjects' suffering under my brother's paw. But now he doesn't have anyone to run to when I return. I can only return triumphant; any other way and Freng will descend into chaos with him on my throne. The other Frenglese kings will squabble over our islands."

And there it was. Emperor Rattarossa trying to murder Jab and then drowning had entrenched Ridgerd even more in his war, with one less voice of reason in his ear. Brouglas's sacrifice might as well have been for nothing. His sword and shield weighed heavily on Jab.

35

SANU

"Brrfl lufflahrk"

- *Vermitch?*

Gentle prodding nudged Sanu out of his uneasy sleep in the tree.

A man's voice below followed. "Brouglas?"

Sanu's eyes snapped open and he nearly fell out of his branch. The pain in his tail came into full focus as he tried to sit up.

"Brouglas?"

Sanu looked down, seeing a pair of soldiers in scout uniforms, both squirrels, one of which held Vermitch's reins.

The style of their leather armor meant they were Nasalid's soldiers. "Are you Brouglas?" the one persisted. "Is this your horse?"

Sanu's mouth and throat felt like he'd taken a mouthful of sand. "N-no. I'm b-borrowing that horse."

"Did a wolf attack you? A badger? Why are you in a tree?" the scout asked. He offered the dull end of a spear.

Sanu uncoiled his tail from the branch and slid down, accepting the assistance and wincing from the pain in his tail. "Hyenas."

"We found your horse and saw the name 'Brouglas' in the saddle. I can read Frenglese letters. How did you come to borrow a Freng's horse? Did you steal it from him?"

The other scout helped Sanu stand. "One less Freng with a warhorse is a good thing on Qawar, I say."

Sanu winced again. "The horse was left to the Sapling of ZelZaytun. She entrusted me with a message to give to Nasalid." Standing up made him lightheaded.

"Bloody tail and a scarred ear?" the first scout said. "You've seen some rough times." He looped his tail around Sanu's arms, helping him balance. "We'll get you to the Liberator. He's on the move from Castle Kraksnout."

Sanu's eyelids felt heavy. "Did he take it?"

"Barely. He left the garrison with strict orders not to loot any of the Sprouters' religious art and trinkets and they almost turned on him."

"That's ... good," Sanu's breathing came heavy. "Strong castle... Nasalid... needs..."

"Easy, easy," the second scout said. "We'll treat your tail and have you back in the saddle. Nobody is bleeding out on us today."

Sanu awoke again, this time in a moving wagon with his tail freshly bandaged and elevated on another cot. His tail didn't hurt as much; the crushing pain had subsided into a dull ache. He was afraid to move it. Above him, wispy clouds passed over. Sanu let out a low moan, unable to move his parched lips.

A shadow passed over him, and somebody helped Sanu sit. His wagon was part of a large convoy— no, an army on the move. In front of him, an older red squirrel sat with his paws in his lap. "Good morning, Sanu." He sported a long beard, with twigs woven into it.

His face tugged at a memory. He knew he'd seen this man before, this Mulcher, but not on Coppergrass. He'd seen him on Qawar.

"I see you look puzzled," the Mulcher said. "My name is Maimon. I am the personal physician of Nasalid. I treated your brother once in much the same way."

"M-Maimon?" Saying the name made Sanu remember meeting him after Nasalid had conquered ZelZaytun. "J-Jab told me you were a philosopher and scientist."

Maimon laughed and the motion made his twigs click together. "Rodents can be many things. I've been wanting to see your brother again. I wanted to tell him that a conversation I had with him inspired me to write a book for perplexed spiritual seekers such as him."

Sanu blinked hard. "I'll tell him when I see him."

"Excellent. How is your tail? The scouts said it was a bite from a hyena. We have ruled out rabies, but we must be vigilant of other infections."

Sanu nodded, pretending he knew what "vigilant" meant. "How can you know?"

Maimon passed a waterskin to him. "Drink. When I told Nasalid that you might die, his response was 'not good enough.' His word is so strong that even infections must obey it. He is eager to see you healthy again."

"Where are we going?" Sanu asked. "I have a message for him."

"We know, the scouts told us. But was it too secret for it to be written down?"

Sanu wanted to let out a chuckle at the awkward moment but knew this wasn't the time for humor. "We couldn't risk the wrong rodents seeing her message."

"I see. Then we should be thankful those hyenas didn't bite a little higher on your spine. I've seen squirrels with tail injuries lose their ability to walk. Now let me see your wound and I can make my next judgment on your treatment."

As Maimon gently undid the bandage, Sanu scanned the area, trying to estimate the number of soldiers. If this was Nasalid's grand army, or what remained of it, they were in trouble. This was barely more than the number of soldiers Ridgerd and Rattarossa had, and Nasalid's entire strategy relied on superior numbers.

And if Dilaal's secret councilors were honest, Nasalid was also running out of resources, which wasn't even factoring in Dilaal's treachery. Ridgerd and Rattarossa might not need to lay siege to ZelZaytun since there might not be anyone left to defend it against them.

When the red squirrel finished, he turned around and tapped the driver on the shoulder. The driver nodded and urged the horses to speed up a bit, pulling the wagon up in the army procession.

Maimon smiled at Sanu. "The wound hasn't spread, but you'll need a cane for a few months. We're speeding up so we can match pace with the Liberator. He's quite interested in what you have to say."

Sanu touched the scar on his ear from where the crossbow bolt had ripped through it back on Coppergrass. He'd had to improvise a cane there for balance, so needing one again didn't seem like the worst news ever. But facing Nasalid after sneaking out of the city twice was another story.

The Gnaverwood towered in the distance, casting a shadow over ZelZaytun, but the holy olive tree's shadow was nothing compared to the storm clouds cast by Nasalid, Rattarossa, and Ridgerd, which had swallowed the whole island.

An island which might never recover from their fight.

36

JAB

Five bitter scholars invited Ganan to a court proceeding with a cruel and wealthy judge. On trial was a thief, caught red-pawed stealing from the judge himself. Before the judge sentenced the thief to die, Ganan stepped up at the academics' invitation. "I would know the thief's name," Ganan said. "Koli," he replied. Ganan turned to the judge. "I had to ask because everyone has only called him 'thief.' Judge, do you know why he stole from you?" The judge folded his arms and coiled his tail. "I do not. What matters is that he did it." Ganan gestured to Koli. "Do you enjoy stealing? Do you have a reason to hate the judge?" The thief shook his head. "No. It was a large house so I assumed there would be money. I lost my job and my father is sick. I need medicine for him. I've never stolen before." Ganan faced the judge and the scholars leaned forward. "In exchange for his life, Koli will return what he stole. You will hire him. A house as large as yours will need a guard. If *you have a spare room, offer it to his father. Treat him them with kindness."*

> *- Excerpt from the Ganandeeds,*
> *"Koli and the Cruel Judge."*

Jab and Yagub stood watch on the hill overlooking ZelZaytun and the deforested lake, where Ridgerd explained his plans to the now-united Sprouter forces. Jab didn't want to be alone after Rattarossa's attack and Yagub already knew the plan, so the two of them agreed to keep lookout.

Yagub whistled at the sight of the Holy City. "It's been a while. You see the tree so much that you forget there's a city around it. Is it true Grovekeepers wouldn't look at the tree while Lady Marjitay's family controlled it?"

Jab nodded. "We didn't have to, but a lot of us chose to. My dad said it was a way to resist them, but my mom said it was almost impossible to do that and keep an eye on kids, so she didn't try. Then she'd say something else to make me and Sanu feel bad about how rowdy we'd get."

"Qawari moms," Yagub laughed. "I wonder if that's where Ridgerd got the idea to not look at the Holy City."

Jab considered remarking how Ridgerd imitated the rodents he was about to kill, but a rumbling in the distance caught his attention.

Horses.

Mounted soldiers.

A whole detachment.

"See that?" Jab asked.

"Yeah, and there's another force coming from the other side. They're going to push us into the lake." Yagub's voice hardened. "We have to tell Ridgerd."

Jab scanned the troops, but they were too far for him to make out much detail. He didn't recognize Nasalid's banner. If only he could get in front of those soldiers and tell them to fetch Nasalid, he could arrange for the Liberator and Ridgerd to have a summit. But without Brouglas, an adult who knew them both, it seemed pointless, and the realization made Jab's heart shrivel.

"You go," Jab said. "I'm going to talk to their commander."

"What? They won't listen to a kid."

"I have to try," Jab said, grabbing the sword and shield of his fallen protector.

"Fine," Yagub seethed, then he stomped down the hill.

Jab ran the other way, toward the Holy City, toward the onrushing soldiers who might trample him. About halfway down the hill, he realized that the horses wouldn't keep charging up such a steep incline, and that he was safer to wait for them to stop on their own. He jumped in place, waving his paws and tail as much as possible, desperate to draw their attention.

Once they came closer, there was no doubt these were Qawari soldiers. Their leather armor, scimitars, and breed of horse said it all. He still couldn't find anyone in the force who carried Nasalid's banner, but there was no way these weren't the Liberator's troops. The left flank actually had a banner carrier, so he repositioned himself so that detachment would see him.

The few hundred horses clopped to a halt at the foot of the hill, and a soldier broke off to approach Jab.

"You're in our way, boy," the soldier called out. "Best be off."

"I have information for Nasalid," Jab called. "The Sprouters are on the other side of the hill. The two kings' armies combined forces and have a single leader now."

The soldier's whiskers stiffened. "Come talk to my commander."

Jab followed him, while the other soldiers fed their horses and sipped water. A gerbil whose helmet sported two hawk feathers to denote his rank rode over from the other detachment.

"Who is the kid?" the gerbil lieutenant asked.

"I have information for Nasalid," Jab replied. "So he's taking me to your commander."

The two soldiers locked eyes with each other, and Jab couldn't guess what kind of unspoken conversation passed between them.

"Nasalid isn't here, I'm afraid."

Jab's heart raced. He'd heard that accent before. The voice belonged to a jird, dressed like a general with four hawk feathers in his helmet and a gold-plated scimitar scabbard attached to his saddle. If he'd been a few years older, Jab might have mistaken him for Nasalid.

"I see how you're looking at me. I take it you've met my brother." Not-Nasalid said. "And I think that means I've met yours. I am Dilaal, mayor of ZelZaytun. I spent some time with Sanu of Rattin recently."

Jab's jaw dropped. "What are you doing here?"

Dilaal motioned to the soldiers around him, many of whom wore slings, eyepatches, and bandages around their legs and chests. "Isn't it obvious? We're here to defeat Rattarossa and Steelfur. My brother has liberated Kraksnout by now, so I will be the one to finish his little war. I tried to reason with King Ridgerd, but he forced my paw."

Jab's neck hair prickled. Something was wrong. "You should know that Rattarossa is dead. Whatever passed between you and Ridgerd before might not matter now. He wants to let his soldiers go home."

"And how does he mean to do that?" Dilaal asked, leaning over his horse. "You can't mean that he's contemplating a surrender?"

Other soldiers nearby pressed in, and their eyes weighed on Jab. He wondered if their interest came from a fear of fighting Ridgerd. By the looks of their injuries, Jab wondered if some of them had fought him already.

"I don't think he's ready to surrender. He wants to get reinforcements so he can lay siege to the city and then have enough troops left over to defend it. I think he's going to try to take over Banuj and use that as a port."

Dilaal stiffened. "If he gets there, he'll meet my brother's warships. I won't let some admiral get the glory of defeating Steelfur. You say he's on the other side of the hill?"

This jird was nothing like his brother. He'd lose most of his troops if he fought Ridgerd now.

"Two times, Ridgerd ran up a hill toward archers. He took both hills, but lost soldiers each time. I don't think he'll do that again." Jab stiffened, standing up as straight as possible. "You can't fight him. You can talk to him though. His weakness is that he has a brother back home who is ruining his kingdom."

Dilaal smirked. "I know something about worthless brothers." He unsheathed his scimitar and lifted it over his head and shouted to his soldiers, "Take position on the hill! Lands and titles to whoever brings me a defeated king!"

Jab had watched Ridgerd rally an army. His voice had come from his belly, and the troops raised fists and weapons in the air with a joyful reply. But Dilaal? He screamed from his throat, making Jab wonder if he'd be able to talk again the rest of the day. What was more striking was the soldiers' response. They mumbled and groaned as they formed position.

Jab couldn't tell if it was fear of Ridgerd or dislike of Dilaal that made the difference.

The scout who'd found Jab offered him a place in the saddle, and Jab accepted, shifting with the weight of Brouglas's sword and shield. Dilaal would need Jab's advice to avoid a bloodbath.

"Is all that true about Ridgerd?" the scout asked. "Is he really invincible?"

"In a fight, he might be," Jab muttered. They'd all find out soon enough.

37

SANU

"Do you think we'll see the Steelfur?"

"On again with this nonsense, are you? Does he visit in your nightmares? He's just a hamster."

"Put Nasalid's mind, the heart of a panther, and the strength of a bear together and you have the Steelfur. I heard that on Coppergrass Isle, he plucked out a porcupine's quill, loaded it into a trumpet, and made it into a blow dart."

"That story sounds more fake than your fiancée."

"She's real! I just haven't met her yet."

— Overheard chatter among Nasalid's forces

Sanu groaned, shifting uncomfortably in the wagon. The bandage on his tail itched so much he thought his hair had turned into spiders. Each bump the wagon hit sent his urge to scratch into a frenzy.

"Deep breaths," Maimon cooed. The red squirrel was a comforting presence, and Sanu understood why Nasalid wanted him around.

On horseback, riding beside the wagon, Nasalid nodded, and the clinks of his chainmail sounded like rainfall, barely audible over the *clop* of his army's horses.

"My brother found a chance to undermine me," Nasalid said. "Sanu, what can you tell me of Ridgerd? How much fight was left in him?"

Sanu adjusted in his seat, still anticipating Nasalid's reprimand for sneaking out of ZelZaytun twice. "When we were in Coppergrass, he told me that he thought he could roll up to the island, show off his army, and you'd give him what he wanted. He also wasn't expecting Rattarossa. Nothing is playing out like he'd planned. I feel like I don't know who he is anymore."

"War changes rodents," Maimon said.

Nasalid gestured toward ZelZaytun. "We won't be stopping in the Holy City. We must intercept my brother before he does something even more rash." He eyed a trumpeter and drummer who rode beside him, and together they played five notes in a slow, booming harmony. The wagon, and the army along with it, veered at a slight angle away from ZelZaytun. Sanu wasn't exactly sure where they were, but he knew they were closer to where Dilaal and Ridgerd met than where Sanu encountered the hyenas.

"Your brother seemed jealous of you," Sanu said. He winced as the words left. That might have been stupid to say.

"I see," Nasalid muttered. "I thought he'd appreciate his appointment. How many councilors did he turn against me?"

Sanu couldn't remember how many met in that prayer hall basement. "I'm not sure, but the rodents I heard from were mad that you didn't let anybody loot, and hated how many trees you cut down. I think the Council of Three didn't know about this group."

Maimon grunted. "I warned you about the trees."

"Arrows save lives and swords risk them," Nasalid said defiantly. "And those warships will keep the shore safe. As for the looting, I won't tarnish the reputation of Grovekeepers. We aren't just fighting for this land, we're fighting for our faith. I won't be sent to the Droughtlands over my subordinates' bad behavior."

Sanu wasn't sure how to ask what "subordinates" meant without sounding dumb. He remembered all the times King Ridgerd confessed his own worries about being sent to the Droughtlands. Getting Dilaal and Ridgerd to sit down had failed, but he might not have that same problem with Nasalid and Ridgerd. But after everything that happened, it didn't seem possible, especially with that Rattarossa monster on the prowl.

Maimon twirled one of his beard twigs. "Your orders make sense to calm and rationally-minded rodents, but those orders come when battle-crazed warriors are neither calm nor thinking rationally."

Nasalid scoffed. "Is that going into your philosophy book?"

"It might, if you permit me to use our conversations," Maimon replied, grinning.

Sanu fought to not scratch his tail. "What are you going to do when you find your brother?"

Nasalid inhaled deeply and stared off into the grasslands ahead of them. "I'll show him and the rest of my troops why the All-Planter put me in charge. I still won't let anyone loot or pillage, but I will remind them why they are to follow me without question." His paw rested on his scimitar. "You should rest, Sanu. Maimon will watch over you. It will be a while before we reach my brother's band of injured cowards."

Hours or days later, Sanu awoke to a wet cloth against his forehead and a fresh bandage around his tail.

Maimon leaned over him and patted his cheek until he opened his eyes.

It was nearly sunset. Or sunrise, he couldn't tell.

The wagon had stopped moving, and the army wasn't surrounding them anymore.

"What happened?" Sanu asked. "Where are we?"

"The site of a battle," Maimon said gravely. "We were too late."

38

JAB

I met a young squirrel named Yagub, a local Qawari who is to be my page. The lad is eager to learn, and he speaks Frenglese astoundingly well. He promised to teach me Qawari, though he was surprised I asked. Why wouldn't I want to know your language and culture, Lord Ganan? (Blessed be You). Yagub isn't fantastic with a sword yet, but I think he'll learn. It's hard not to miss my brother now that I have a younger rodent beside me.

- From the prayer journal of Sir Brouglas

Jab believed the All-Planter had a plan for everyone. He couldn't understand how or why that plan involved Jab returning to this cursed lake. Without trees or animals, it looked appropriately dead for what had happened there, and what was about to happen again. Yagub would've had time to tell Ridgerd that these Grovekeeper forces were coming, maybe believing that Nasalid himself was leading the charge instead of the glory-seeking impostor of a brother.

At least Jab had Brouglas's sword and shield.

Sharing a horse with a scout, they summited the hill.

"Bows ready!" Dilaal shouted at the soldiers, most of whom hadn't even reached the top yet. His voice was squeaky and hoarse.

On the other side of the hill, rows of heavily armored Sprouter soldiers clambered up. Ridgerd must have ordered the charge early.

"Fire!" Dilaal shouted again, even though barely any of his troops had drawn their bows.

"What's he thinking?" the scout muttered. Jab tensed. This would end poorly. Dilaal had to be stopped.

"Let me down," Jab said. He leaned forward to dismount, but got a better look at Ridgerd's forces coming uphill, defying the thin line of arrows pelting them. Brouglas's shield pushed into his stomach.

There weren't enough Sprouter soldiers to be Ridgerd's full force, especially considering the addition of Rattarossa's troops. Coming closer, he noticed the similar contour of their armor. Jab's blood ran cold. These were the Barkhearts, the fiercest warriors come to fight Dilaal's weakened, injured, tired, and demoralized force.

As the Barkhearts climbed, the outlines of their steel armor and devilbeaks came into clearer focus. He did not want to see a line of them fight.

"Fire!" Dilaal shout-squeaked.

Jab hopped off the horse to the scout's protest. Either Ridgerd was going to surround them with his main force or he'd made an escape. But these Barkhearts weren't regular soldiers.

The first wave of knights summited the hill, and seeing them up close amid a crowd of Grovekeepers, Jab realized why they scared him so much. At the first lake battle months ago, a pawful of Sprouter knights had brutally defended themselves against overwhelming odds. They fought both tactically and savagely. They had been Barkheart knights and Jab hadn't realized it until now. Their savagery was the source of Jab's nightmares.

"Switch to clubs!" Jab shouted. He had impersonated an officer once before, but he didn't think he'd need to bother this time.

"Yeah!" someone else called. "Bludgeon them."

"Droughtlands!" another soldier yelped. "Barkhearts!"

A few soldiers in front of Jab broke ranks and careened down the opposite side of the hill, before the entire force had even arrived. Jab weaved through horses and soldiers, trying to get to Dilaal, or at least a trumpeter. He clutched Brouglas's equipment tight, as if squeezing heavy things could make him faster.

Thuds banged against metal, and swords cracked bone. Horses screamed, knocking their already-injured riders off. There couldn't have been more than a few dozen Barkhearts, and they were already making a dent in Dilaal's weakened troops.

Screams and whinnies, *whumps* and crunches filled Jab's ears.

Bloody memories streaked through Jab's mind and he couldn't tell what was his imagination and what was real anymore. He caught a glimpse of a Barkheart's helmet, and he could've sworn he saw glowing red eyes through it.

The Divine Poetics talked about Pruning Day. The All-Planter would send fearsome warriors to purge the islands of the wicked rodents. Had they come for Dilaal? Or maybe they'd come for Jab, exacting judgment for all his weaknesses, all his lies, all the deaths he'd been powerless to stop.

Jab's breathing caught and he bumped into a horse, which stomped on his hindpaw.

The metal-shod hoof snapped something in his hindpaw but Jab couldn't breathe deeply enough to howl in pain.

He couldn't find Dilaal. So much noise.

These Barkhearts were here for blood and glory, not prisoners and resolution.

He couldn't find Sanu or Ridgerd. Brouglas wasn't here to save him again.

So much death.

A Barkheart nearby swung his devilbeak, unhorsing a rider from his saddle. The rider fell to the ground with a gasp, and the horse reared, but the knight attacked the horse, which swayed and tilted toward Jab.

The wall of fine hair and thick muscle fell on Jab, pinning him into the ground.

The horse didn't deserve to die.

Jab's memories became noisier than the battle unfolding around him.

His breath caught in his throat.

He had imagined he'd be reunited with his parents in the Walled Garden, and Kash too. But this was Pruning Day, and he was on the wrong side.

Qawar was lost. Nasalid had destroyed the land in trying to save the people, and Ridgerd slaughtered the rodents to claim the land.

Everything went dark as Jab struggled to reposition his shield.

His last thought was of his brother.

I'm sorry, Sanu.

39

SANU

General Ironseed surrendered to the Frenglese invaders today. I wonder what will become of me. I don't know if my account will survive, but I know this: those Barkheart Order knights emerged from the blackest pits of the Droughtlands. There will never be peace in Qawar as long as they persist here.

- Diaries of General Ironseed's secretary

Sanu was in a fresh graveyard. All around him, soldiers and horses lay scattered across the hilltop.

With some difficulty, he stood, ignoring the burning pain in his tail. "What happened?"

Beside him, Maimon shook his head. "There was a battle here. Hard to say who won."

Sanu scanned the area, watching Nasalid's troops inspect the dead. "Did they all die?"

"No, no," Maimon said. "Other physicians are tending to the severely wounded at the bottom of the hill. "We're looking for survivors who can't move. Horses too."

"Did Rattarossa do this?" Sanu's breath caught. "Or King Ridgerd?"

"We don't know who ordered the attack. Come on down." Maimon offered Sanu a cane, and then he hopped off the side of the wagon, extending a paw for Sanu to grab. "There are some Sprouter survivors, and we could use another Frenglese speaker. Even better if you know Rottelander."

Wincing, Sanu wasn't about to ask how Maimon knew that Sanu had learned Frenglese.

Nasalid's troops hefted wounded horses and soldiers, slowly clearing the way and making the grass visible. Seeing these casualties reminded Sanu of when he and Jab buried their parents before they got involved with this conflict. They'd picked a grassy hill like this one, which looked out at ZelZaytun, so their parents could have some access to the Holy City in death. Sanu wondered if dying this close to ZelZaytun was a comfort to some of these soldiers. Remembering the Sprouters' pilgrim mentality, he wondered how many felt that way on both sides.

"Sanu!" The voice belonged to Nasalid, a few yards away.

Maimon helped Sanu hobble over. His balance was messed up from his tail injury, but not in the same way as when he'd lost part of his ear in Coppergrass. Nasalid and a lieutenant were crouched over a fallen soldier. Getting closer, Sanu's heart raced.

It wasn't just a fallen soldier. It was a Barkheart knight.

Dents littered his steel armor, and tufts of fur poked through the joints.

Nasalid's lieutenant removed the Barkheart's helmet, revealing a dormouse, whose fur was browner than Rattarossa's. Blood matted his fur in several spots, and his breathing was labored.

Nasalid glanced at Sanu. "Tell him we'll make him comfortable in exchange for information."

Sanu nodded. "This is Nasalid. He said he'd make you comfortable if you give him information. He's a rodent of his word."

The dormouse coughed. His response was so accented and raspy that Sanu could only understand the word for "Rottelander."

"I only speak Frenglese and Qawari," Sanu lamented.

The dormouse coughed again, some blood gushing out of his mouth. He glanced at Maimon and scowled. "Tell Nasalid ... go to the Droughtlands."

"He won't talk, Nasalid," Sanu said.

"Tell him I can bury him near the Gnaverwood or let the crows get to him here," Nasalid said flatly.

Sanu inched backward and translated, reminding the Barkheart that Nasalid was true to his word.

The dormouse sighed. "What does he want to know?"

"Where are the kings?" Sanu asked.

"Rattarossa is dead. Ridgerd has moved south with the main force."

After Sanu relayed the information to Nasalid, the Liberator nodded to his lieutenant. "Remove his armor, take his weapons, and treat him with the other wounded ones."

"Liberator!" a voice called some distance away. "Come quick!"

Nasalid motioned for Sanu and Maimon to follow, and he approached the calling voice.

Sitting in the grass was another jird, holding his knees tight to his chest, rocking back and forth. A dead horse sat to his left, and a squirrel's tail poked out from under it.

"Dilaal," Nasalid ground out.

The tail underneath the horse twitched. "Someone's under there!" Sanu said.

Nasalid glanced over his shoulder at the pinned-down tail. "Come on, men, let's free him." A team of soldiers came over and struggled against the animal's dead weight. The soldiers were careful to avoid the tail, and dug their hindpaws into the ground for leverage, shoving and straining against the creature's body. Nasalid pushed up his chainmail sleeves and joined them, and Maimon came in too. Sanu hobbled over and shoved his cane under the horse's stomach for a lever.

"One big heave," Nasalid said, and the team pushed off the horse.

Beneath it was a Qawari boy, clutching a shield over his torso, gasping for breath.

It was Jab, holding Brouglas's shield.

Jab!

Heart racing, Sanu dove into the grass beside his brother. "Jab!" Sanu cried. "Can you hear me?" Delicately, Sanu removed the shield from Jab's grip. Sanu wondered why his brother had a Sprouter knight's shield, but now wasn't the time for questions.

"Maimon!" Nasalid shouted.

"On it." The red squirrel crouched beside Jab. He pinched Jab's nostrils, opened Jab's mouth, and breathed, puffing up Jab's chest. "Sit him up straight," Maimon ordered.

"Will he live?" Nasalid asked, voice cracking. "Tell me he'll live, Maimon."

Sanu's knees buckled. He thought he'd watched Jab die once before. They'd come too far for it to happen for real. Sanu pulled his brother's limp body into a hug. Maimon and Nasalid's stronger arms pushed Jab upright.

"Jab ... don't leave me."

A furry tail pressed against Sanu's neck, followed by Jab's breath.

In between wheezes, the reply came. "We've ... done that ... enough times."

Sanu hugged Jab tighter.

Two more knees joined them in the grass. Nasalid wrapped his arms over the brothers' shoulders. "The All-Planter provides." A teardrop wet Sanu's scalp.

Mighty Nasalid, Liberator of ZelZaytun, the mighty ruler and great unifier, wept at the brothers' reunion.

After a deep breath, Nasalid rose again. "Now I must deal with *my* brother."

40

JAB

Lord Ganan said, "Two farmers' lands bordered each other. One lost many crops to fruit bats each night. He set up a grand net over his crops, and the bats couldn't get through. Frustrated, the bats returned to their cave, not knowing another farm lay close by. But without their dung to fertilize, the first farmer's crops soon shriveled anyway." Ganan's followers pressed Him. "What does that mean? Is the lesson with the bats or the farmers?" "Discover for yourself."

- Excerpt from the Ganandeeds, "The Parable of the Fruit Bat."

Maybe he was delirious from the pain in his damaged hindpaw, but Jab had known Sanu was alive. He never doubted it for half a second since they parted ways. But being reunited with him was such a relief. Maybe that relief came in part due to the soldiers removing a dead horse off his body, but he couldn't be happier, despite the knowledge that every rib was probably cracked and it felt like he was breathing in glass. Sanu didn't look much better with his bandaged tail and cane.

Seeing Nasalid also lifted Jab's spirits, but it meant that Ridgerd and Nasalid were now physically closer than ever. From his seated position on the hilltop, Jab surveyed the area, not entirely sure who won the battle. Collapsed suits of Barkheart armor lay strewn across the hill, standing out from the Grovekeeper forces only because of their reflective steel armor.

Dilaal was one of the few survivors, but as the jird stood to meet Nasalid, Jab saw the truth in his eyes. Dilaal would return to this battle in his nightmares. Jab wondered if he'd been carrying around that look himself for months since his first battle.

A few of Nasalid's fresh troops made a circle around Nasalid and Dilaal, while the others continued searching for survivors. Maimon crouched between Jab and Sanu, listening to Jab's breathing.

Nasalid glared at his brother. "You undermined me." His tone was even. "You forced soldiers to march who weren't ready. You called for an attack before they were ready. History will remember this as the final battle of the Barkheart Order and you as the general who defeated them, but I think you can see a different result."

A tremor ran through Dilaal's body. "Are you going to kill me then?" He hung his head low, as if exposing his neck for a scimitar.

Nasalid placed his paws on Dilaal's shoulders. "You're still my brother. I'd rather have you live with what happened here. You defeated the last two hundred Barkhearts in Qawar at the cost of one-thousand soldiers, rodents with families and hopes."

Dilaal stared at his hindpaws. "I'm sorry."

"There are another thousand who need that apology more. Take them back to ZelZaytun. Earn their trust and mine back. With the Barkhearts dealt with, you may have paved the way for a greater success." Nasalid's voice became grave. "But know the cost of your victory."

Jab shuddered, which sent a wave of pain through his ribs. This was what Ridgerd had wanted to avoid. This was what Jab and Sanu had wanted to avoid. The word 'victory' didn't feel appropriate.

At least it wasn't Pruning Day.

Nasalid embraced Dilaal. Jab couldn't remember the last time he'd seen two grown men hug. He remembered the sadness in Brouglas's prayer journal, how he wrote about missing his brother, and those things he said about trying to contact him. Brouglas would never get that hug. And maybe if Ridgerd could be convinced he could get that hug with *his* estranged brother, this would all be resolved. Jab almost laughed at himself, imagining telling a king to call off a war in exchange for a hug.

But then, it wasn't as crazy as a king jumping into a lake wearing metal armor.

Maimon cleared his throat. "Jab, it seems like your breathing is labored. Let's get you into the wagon and we can examine you. Do you feel ready to walk?"

Beside him, Sanu grabbed his cane and struggled to stand, then he offered a paw for Jab to do the same.

Groaning with the effort, Jab stood, using his tail to hold himself upright. He'd need medical attention for his hindpaw. His lungs were filled with knives. Or scimitars. He took a step and realized it was knives and scimitars and at least five rocks.

A team of soldiers helped Jab into a wagon, and Maimon climbed inside, laying Jab down.

"A mobile triage wagon was an old tactic by General Ironseed," Maimon said. "Say what you will about him, but among history's generals, he lost the fewest men to disease and infection. I'm going to examine your ribs. You definitely have some cracked bones, but with the proper bandages, you'll be on the mend. I'll give you something for the pain."

Sanu entered the wagon and squatted beside Jab. "Yeah, his medicine is good."

Jab decided not to remind Sanu that Maimon had healed him before, mostly because Maimon's inspection hurt so much he couldn't keep his eyes open. Maimon released some pressure, and Jab gasped for air.

He opened his eyes to the sight of a leafy paste near his snout.

"It tastes like hindpaws, but it will dull the ache," Maimon said.

Jab would've preferred hindpaws to the monstrosity on that spoon. His mouth dried, clenching worse than when he told lies.

Nasalid came to the wagon and placed a paw on the side, eyeing Jab and Sanu. "Maimon, are they safe to travel?"

Maimon shot him a stern look. "That depends on where you want to take these children who are too young for war."

Nasalid scrunched his snout, tangling his whiskers. "I don't think I can reason with King Ridgerd without them."

Sanu struggled to sit straight. "Maimon, Nasalid knows that if you send me to ZelZaytun, I'll sneak out again."

Jab groaned from the pain in his chest. "We're staying with Nasalid if he'll have us."

Maimon sighed. "This is a risk to their health."

"Every second those invaders are on this island is a risk to everyone," Nasalid said.

Jab propped himself on an elbow to a half-sit position. Looking into Nasalid's eyes, he understood. "You're going to show us to King Ridgerd, aren't you? Show him how his fight has ruined Qawar."

Nasalid shook his head. "I won't use you like tools. I'm running out of trustworthy translators. You both almost got him to back down, as individuals. I think the time for solving our dispute with weapons is at an end. You two will be the heroes. You will be remembered as the guardians of the holy Gnaverwood grove."

"Grove guardians," Jab muttered. He could put off a long rest if it meant getting Ridgerd and Nasalid to talk as reasonable leaders.

The Barkhearts and Rattarossa were gone, so the only remaining challenge was the conflict in the king's own heart.

41

SANU

"Did you hear Rattarossa drowned in ZelZaytun's lake?"

"That's ridiculous."

"One of his soldiers mutinied, I bet, and shoved him in. Or Ridgerd Steelfur wanted to remove a rival."

"Ridgerd Steelfur isn't like that."

"Ha! Know him well, do you? Did your parents invite him over for sheltercake when you were a kid?"

"I bet Rattarossa was killed by angry spirits."

"Don't get all superstitious on us."

"No, I bet it was angry spirits from the Battle of Phranktonbourg. They chased him across the sea for his atrocities."

— Overheard chatter among Nasalid's forces

FAMILIES BROKEN

For Sanu, watching Jab observe the scenery around the lake hurt almost as much as his own tail. Maimon had insisted on a slower pace for the wagon than the rest of the army, and Nasalid's banner had faded in the distance among the horde of troops.

Watching Jab shiver tore Sanu's heart out. Sanu had bad nightmares about the siege of ZelZaytun and the castle on Coppergrass, but whatever Jab had experienced at this lake had broken him. Almost drowning in the ocean and washing ashore on Coppergrass might have been a factor in his constant nightmares too.

"I'm worried about Ridgerd," Sanu said, desperate to bring Jab out of his trance.

Jab sighed. "Me too. I wasn't sure how to tell you this, but Rattarossa didn't jump in the lake like everyone is saying."

"I *knew* that sounded fake." Sanu smirked. "So what happened?"

"He attacked me..." Jab stared at Sanu, the pain in his eyes suggesting the story he wanted to tell had more words than he wanted to say. After a sigh, Jab added, "but Sir Brouglas defended me. He fought off Rattarossa and told me to run, but—"

The beaver knight had saved both of their lives and been the voice of reason in Ridgerd's ear. Sanu's throat tightened, unsure where this was going. Brouglas might have been acting nobly, but killing a king would not go over well in any court. "You don't have to say it," Sanu replied. "He's been thrown in a dungeon."

Jab winced. "You don't understand. He told me to run, and, and I didn't. I tried to help him. He got distracted and—"

The wagon hit a bump, making Sanu aware of his surroundings. Maimon sat with the driver, scribbling something on parchment. Nasalid's army had mostly passed them at their faster marching speed, and the wagon had wheeled past the lake now.

After a deep breath, Jab met Sanu's eyes again. "Rattarossa ... cut off Brouglas's wrist. Rattarossa beat him b-because I distracted him. He wanted to save me, but I put him in more danger."

Tears welled under Sanu's eyelids. Brouglas was their protector. He couldn't have lost to a brute like Rattarossa. "So he's recovering now?"

"No, Sanu... Rattarossa tried to kill me again, and Brouglas tackled him, forcing him into the lake from a pier. They were both in metal armor."

Seeing Brouglas's sword and shield tied a knot in his stomach, knowing that the brave knight had saved Jab one more time, even after his death. Sanu buried his face in his paws. Not only had they lost a protector and mentor, but Ridgerd had lost a calm voice that he trusted.

"It's silly," Jab said, "but I'd begun to think of Brouglas as an uncle or even a fatherly kind of guy. Nobody could replace Dad, but Brouglas really took care of us."

Maimon cleared his throat loudly. After a sigh, Jab added, "Much like kind Maimon has bandaged my hindpaw and given me medicine so I can walk again."

Sanu nodded. "I don't think I want to be a soldier anymore if this is what war looks like."

Jab gestured toward the landscape. "Hard to see past the soldiers, but at least we're away from the lake."

"What about Yagub?"

"He's all right," Jab replied. "But he was starting to worry me. He seemed to idolize the Barkhearts. I think it's awful to say but I'm kind of glad they're gone."

"It doesn't sound awful," Sanu said. "It's awful Yagub had still wanted to join them. But he's safe?"

"Safe enough to tell Ridgerd that Nasalid is on his tail. We were at that hill and saw Dilaal coming up, though we didn't know exactly who it was at first. I went to warn them about Ridgerd, and he ran the other direction to warn Ridgerd about them."

"He let you?"

Jab shrugged, then held his chest. "I didn't ask his permission."

Maimon placed his parchment on the bench and glanced over his shoulder at Sanu and Jab. "Get some rest, boys. That's the only thing Nasalid and I can agree on. We'll have time to catch up later. I'll wake you for your prayers and food."

They were away from the lake, so Sanu knew Jab would be able to relax again. Sanu wasn't sure if he could rest, knowing Brouglas was at the bottom of that lake, but he knew the old beaver would scold him if he didn't try. They did have his sword and shield, plus their dad's old scimitar.

42

JAB

Almighty All-Planter, I've had it explained to me by intellectuals, seedlings, and my parents, yet I don't think I'll ever wrap my head around why you allow rodents capacity for such cruelty. Until I understand it, I will take it as your invitation to be more kind and generous. I hope I can ease some of the pain in the Great Sea.

- From the prayer journal of Sir Brouglas

Prayers recited, breakfast eaten, bodies aching, Jab and Sanu rattled along as the wagon approached Nasalid's war tent. Jab had never been to this area of Qawar before, but knew they were near the isthmus leading to Banuj, a fishing port. He once pretended to be from there for a mission, and remembering the lie shriveled up his little positivity boost from praying.

The scrapes of tools on wood from working carpenters and *clangs* of blacksmiths toiling at anvils provided enough noise in the camp to discourage Jab from talking to Sanu and Maimon.

Nasalid stormed from the tent, the flap whipping open. He pointed a stiff finger at Sanu. "Are you positive you translated correctly from that Barkheart?"

Jab stared at his brother, shocked that Sanu had spoken to a Barkheart on Nasalid's behalf.

"Y-yes," Sanu stammered. "He said Ridgerd was going to Banuj."

"Then where is he?" Nasalid demanded. A blacksmith plunged a hot blade into water, and the steamy hiss added force to Nasalid's question. "We've searched the town. It's as empty as we left it when we evacuated the ports. The only signs of life are our own warships near the harbor."

Jab breathed deeply, wincing from the pain in his chest. "The last thing King Ridgerd said when I was around him was that he wanted to take a port so he could send for reinforcements. Sanu didn't mess up."

Nasalid rubbed his temples and coiled his tail. "Then perhaps our opponent is more clever than I'd thought. He told the Barkhearts one thing, and sent them off to die, knowing one of them would give up his secrets. He then went somewhere else before his decoys knew the truth." Nasalid almost sounded intrigued.

"He could be anywhere," Jab said. "I'm sorry I don't know anything else."

Sanu's eyes widened. "He's playing double siege with you."

"What do you mean?" The force of Nasalid's voice seemed to silence the workers in the camp.

"I played him once," Sanu said. "He sees warfare like a strategy game. He made you think he was going to one place. He's preparing for another strike somewhere else."

As the smell of chipped wood and smoke twirled in Jab's nostrils, his heart raced at the idea, though the rational part of his mind told him that there weren't many places for Ridgerd to go. Jab remembered why he and Sanu decided to keep separating—one of them always said something stupid to get them both in trouble.

"So where is he going?" Nasalid demanded. "To ZelZaytun?"

"No," Jab said, feeling the carpenters and blacksmiths leaning toward them. "He said he wouldn't take the city if he couldn't defend it. Most of his soldiers think they're pilgrims and will leave Qawar once he captures the city."

Sanu struggled to stand. "He can't defend it against *you*. He's playing double siege, Nasalid. He's going to come for you directly."

Maimon grunted. "You've been so worried about his sword, you've neglected his mind. That is a costly mistake, Liberator."

Nasalid's tail fell limp into the sparse grass. "And my main force is searching Banuj." He spun around and called to a scout, "Bring them back here at once. Tell them to be hyper vigilant and expect treachery."

The scout saluted him and galloped away.

Nasalid unsheathed his scimitar. "So, the general will attack the general. Quite the bold strategy, I must say. These camp followers are in danger." He faced the main body of the camp, inhaled deeply, and boomed, "All of you, get into Banuj! Trade places with the soldiers. I'm expecting an attack from the rear. Blacksmiths and carpenters who can swing a hammer, you lot stay and arm yourselves with the largest hammers you can find. You'll fare better against their armor with those than a blade."

The camp followers were rodents of all ages. They grabbed supplies, stuffed them into pawcarts, and rushed out of camp.

The rearguard formed up around Nasalid, maces in paw.

Maimon hopped out of the triage wagon and shoved a stiff finger in Nasalid's face. "I have been loyal to you; I've brought you out of death's clutches a full three times now, and I've given you solid advice. You must let me take those boys to safety."

"Don't let him, Nasalid!" Jab pleaded. "We have to talk to Ridgerd or he'll never stop."

"Yeah, we won't run fast, but we will run from you the first chance we get if you take us away," Sanu added.

Nasalid pointed to his tent. "Boys, get in there. If a battle comes, I don't want you two in the crossfire."

Maimon opened his mouth to protest, but Jab and Sanu were already halfway out of the wagon. Breathing hurt, and Sanu had to lean heavily on his cane, but they were out of that thing fast, hobbling over to Nasalid's tent.

Tugging on his beard, Maimon scowled. "I won't let my patients out of my care. And you must promise me you won't get involved with the fighting."

Jab shook his head. "We've had enough battles. I don't want to get in another one."

Rumbling came like a thundercloud in the distance.

It wasn't weather, but a different force of nature.

Ridgerd marched toward Nasalid's camp, with hundreds, maybe thousands of warriors at his back. For the first time in their conflict together, Nasalid didn't outnumber Ridgerd's troops. Nasalid also didn't have the arrows to bury Ridgerd's troops.

"Crossbows ready!" Nasalid roared. "Aim for the joints. We'll make them regret not choosing the sea."

Jab wasn't about to let anyone else die. "We need something to make them stop." He straightened his back, which felt like a stab wound. "There's got to be something in here we can use."

43

SANU

One of the Frenglese nobles approached me today. He said if I forswore Grovekeeping, he'd let me live and I could work for him, since he needed a scribe literate in Qawari. What can I say? I know there is a special place in the Walled Garden for those who keep the faith in the muzzle of death, but the All-Planter only gave me one life, and I intend to keep it.

- Diaries of General Ironseed's secretary

Sanu admired his brother's courage. "You're right. We have to stop them."

Maimon stepped in front of the war tent's flap. "You are not leaving this tent!"

"Maimon, you can't possibly want anyone to die." Jab massaged the bandages over his chest and hindpaw.

"Exactly," the red squirrel said. "Least of all, two young boys with their whole lives ahead of them."

Shouts came from outside, followed by the clang of steel on steel. At close range, Nasalid's crossbows could puncture Sprouter armor, but it might not be enough. Sanu peeked out the tent's open window flap. Nasalid's guards had formed three lines. One line had taken a knee to fire their crossbows, a second stood to fire over their heads, and a third reloaded. Ridgerd's soldiers either fell or staggered as the bolts flew.

"Shields, lads!" Ridgerd's voice outside shook the tent as much as the charging hindpaws.

"Nasalid's main force will arrive soon," Maimon said. "There are no clouds in the sky. The Sprouters will tire themselves out in their heavy armor, and Nasalid will carry the day, given time."

Sanu clenched his fist, which also made his wounded tail hurt, because everything made it hurt. He opened his mouth to speak, but the orchestra of crossbow bolts slamming against metal shields was deafening. They were at close range.

When the crossbow barrage ended, Nasalid's voice carried over the fray. "Maces! Aim for heads and stomachs. Defend your home! Defend the Holy City!"

Sanu poked his head out the window flap and shouted, "Stop fighting!"

But it didn't matter. Once the crossbows had stopped, Ridgerd emerged from behind his shield and swung his sword. His own war cries mixed with the noise of blades ripping through leather and maces hammering armor made Sanu's shout a whisper.

Maimon yanked on Sanu's good ear, pulling him away from the window. "I'm trying to help you! Stop being so stubborn."

Jab was already at the tent flap. "Sorry, Maimon."

The red squirrel released his grip on Sanu and pounced toward Jab, spryer than Sanu would've guessed. He grabbed Jab by the tail. "You'll give me a heart attack. If you have even an ounce of respect for either Ridgerd or Nasalid, you'll stay out of it. Jab, you said yourself that Sir Brouglas died because you distracted him. Are you so eager to repeat mistakes?"

Sanu glanced out the window again. Blood coated Ridgerd's sword. Many more of Nasalid's guards had fallen than Ridgerd's troops. The Liberator continued giving orders as Steelfur cut his way closer, ripping through Nasalid's soldiers like paper.

"Are you willing to let Nasalid lose then?" Sanu asked. "Look for yourself."

When Maimon looked out the window, Sanu glanced over his shoulder at Jab, who was hoisting the shield and sword he got from Brouglas. Sanu stepped backward and grabbed the sword.

"We're going out there," Sanu said. "We can protect ourselves. Jab can lift the shield and I can swing the sword to deflect. I learned how to fight from Sprouter knights and Jab learned how to stay alive from Grovekeeper scouts. We promise to come back alive so you can yell at us." Instead of waiting for a response, the brothers backed toward the tent flap. Sanu didn't love pointing a sword at an old timer who had saved his life, but they needed to get out there and try to stop the fighting before Nasalid died.

Maimon's whiskers drooped. "I'm going with you then."

By the time they came outside, Nasalid's line of soldiers had fallen back, and Ridgerd's forces pressed forward, so where Sanu and Jab had been closer to Nasalid, now they were closer to the back of Ridgerd's troops.

"Let's go," Sanu said, pointing toward the front line of Ridgerd's troops.

Jab lifted the shield, letting the wide end protect both of them.

Maimon took a giant step backward, and three Sprouter soldiers popped up from the side, spears raised.

Sanu cursed himself. Of *course*, some soldiers would check the war tent. "We need to talk to King Ridgerd," Sanu said.

The biggest of the three Sprouters wiggled his spear near Sanu's eyes. "What are two kids and a Mulcher doing in a tent?"

"Nasalid will have a summit with the king," Jab said, lowering the shield. "Do any of you recognize me? I'm the squirrel who was tagging along with the king's forces. Sir Brouglas, the beaver knight, was protecting me."

One of the other knights nudged the big one. "It's him. Or the other one. Remember they said he had a twin brother?"

"Fine," big guy said. "Who's the Mulcher?"

Maimon folded his arms over his chest. "Their physician. Nasalid appointed me to watch over them. Now take us to the king!"

War shouts and death screams punctured the sun-roasted air.

"He's a bit busy at the moment," big guy said.

Sanu had to shield his eyes with his paw when looking at them, since the sun was reflecting off their helmets.

"Boys, translate for me," Maimon said. "Tell them that Ridgerd will collapse from heat exhaustion under all that armor. Jab here told me you lost more brothers-in-arms to dehydration and heat exhaustion than arrows and maces."

Sanu translated, and the guards lowered their spears a fraction.

"Ridgerd hasn't taken a break since this all started," Jab insisted. "He's done most of the fighting."

Sanu lowered his sword and approached big guy. "So, what'll it be? Will you be the ones who can be blamed for the king dying here or will you be the ones honored for ending this war?"

After exchanging some looks with the other two, big guy nodded. "We'll take you to him."

Relief flooded Sanu, but it dammed up immediately. The ground shook and new shouts joined the fray with the thundering of hooves.

Nasalid's reinforcements had arrived.

44

JAB

> Ganan flexed his tail and twitched his ears. "You see by my red fur and squirrel body that I was born a Mulcher. You can see by the twigs in my beard that I still consider myself one. If you would follow me, I do not ask that you tangle twigs and pretend to be something you are not. I ask that you create a society where there is no division between enemy and friend and no difference between rich and poor. Rodents most often ask me about the Walled Garden. Bring the Walled Garden to this life instead of hoping to arrive there in the next. Put aside your differences and love each other. It is both the simplest and most difficult thing I ask."
>
> - Excerpt from the Ganandeeds, "The Farewell."

Jab limped as fast as his injured hindpaw would allow, next to his also-injured brother and an angry Maimon. Three spear-carrying Sprouter knights escorted them toward the front line.

Nasalid's reinforcements had arrived, charging at King Ridgerd's rearguard. Spotting Ridgerd himself was simple enough since the other soldiers gave him a wide berth, focusing on his other warriors, who still put up a fight. The heavy steel armor reflected the harsh sunlight.

The biggest of the Sprouter soldiers escorting them nudged Maimon. "You don't have any water, do you?"

"He doesn't speak Frenglese," Jab said. He didn't think it would be polite to add that the soldier's voice was so raspy and dry that Jab could barely understand him.

Soldiers from both sides fell, cascading into each other like tidal waves with scimitars against armored rocks. Nasalid was losing soldiers faster, but Ridgerd had fewer rodents to lose.

Sanu pointed at a troop of advancing riders, all of whom had their maces and clubs out for battle. They were heading for their group.

Jab grabbed Maimon's paw, tugged him in front of the group, and dropped his shield.

Sanu dropped the sword and did the same. "Drop your spears and tell them you surrender. We'll get to the front faster that way."

As Jab and Sanu came closer, Nasalid's main force converged from two sides on Ridgerd's troops, pinning them into a circle.

The riders approaching them skidded to a stop, and behind them, Jab caught a glimpse of other Sprouter soldiers kneeling in the dirt without a weapon in front of them and their helmets removed. Ridgerd's soldiers were surrendering.

Jab waved his tail over his head to catch the riders' attention. "We have news for the Liberator! These soldiers with us have surrendered."

Sanu echoed Jab's message in Qawari. When the soldiers protested, Sanu asked, "Would you rather fake a surrender or spend your days as a prisoner?"

When Nasalid's riders acknowledged Jab, one of them asked, "What is this news for Nasalid? He is busy."

"Ridgerd Steelfur will fight to the death. He'll take most of the army down with him. We can get him to stop fighting."

The rider's horse neared Jab, and all the fur on his body stood on end. A horse had nearly killed him, and an image of the short-haired heavy animal falling toward him flashed through his mind. He shook his head. No more nightmares. He needed to be fine and stable around horses. "Come on," the rider insisted, extending a paw. "I'll take you."

The other two riders offered paws to Sanu and Maimon, who accepted them with the grace of an injured squirrel and a man with creaky joints.

"You three," the rider said, indicating the freshly-surrendered Sprouters, "Thank you for watching over these three. Go over there and you will be shown mercy as a peaceful prisoner. You'll get passage to the Freng Islands or Rotteland."

The rider kicked the horse, and they took off, giving Jab more details of the unfolding battle.

Ridgerd had so many bodies piled around him that the rodents he fought had to step over them to get close to him, and Ridgerd's remaining fighters had similar piles accumulating. More and more of Nasalid's soldiers fell. But two of Ridgerd's fighters dropped to the ground without being struck by a mace or crossbow bolt, and the royal hamster's heavy breathing was louder than the surrounding noise of battle.

"Heat exhaustion," Sanu muttered.

The ring of troops flanking Ridgerd's soldiers broke apart, scattering as Nasalid's rodents fell by Ridgerd's paw or fled it.

They were close enough now for Jab to make out the contours of the king's crown helmet. It made him even more distinguishable, but also carried the symbolic weight of his authority.

King Ridgerd swung his sword, knocking another one of Nasalid's soldiers into the dirt. Then he sank to a knee and planted his sword in the ground, holding on to the hilt like a cane even though he wasn't walking.

Chest screaming, Jab leapt off the saddle and hobbled forward, and Sanu did the same. Both brothers cried out, "Ridgerd!"

Nasalid's remaining soldiers parted, and the Liberator appeared, holding a crossbow.

"Nasalid!" Jab cried. "Don't!"

Ridgerd's breathing came so heavy and labored that Jab heard it over his own pained breaths.

Shoulders heaving, Ridgerd turned, eyes widening at the sight of Sanu and Jab.

Nasalid's jaw dropped, and a breeze rustled his fur.

Nasalid shook his head and removed Ridgerd's helmet. He unsheathed his scimitar, the steel catching a glint of the victorious sun, and placed his sharp blade at the king's neck. The jird's gaze left the hamster, moving to the remaining Sprouter soldiers. In waves, they dropped their weapons and sank to their knees.

"Ridgerd Steelfur," Nasalid said. "I refused to meet with you before, because I believe it is dishonorable to meet a rodent I intend to kill."

"Don't do it!" Jab yelled.

"His kingdom will fall apart!" Sanu added. "How many more lives do you want to ruin?"

Nasalid glared at the boys, but his eyes dropped a hair's width, as if noticing their bandages and the pain this conflict had forced on them.

Nasalid turned his gaze back to Ridgerd and sheathed his scimitar. "Someone translate for me. Ridgerd, I see no dishonor in meeting you now. Let's get you out of that armor and into the shade. You all must be dreadfully hot."

Ridgerd's lips were so dry they looked white and his voice came out like a croak. "Boys, t-translate for me."

Soldiers got out of the way and let Jab and Sanu come over.

"T-tell him I understand Qawari but I cannot speak it. I cannot surrender."

Jab coiled his tail. "I won't tell him that."

"It's not a surrender," Sanu said. "He said he'll meet with you. Maybe you two could come up with a peace treaty instead."

Ridgerd winced. His breathing came so ragged that Jab worried he'd fall over and die. "A t-treaty. That s-sounds—"

The king fell face first into the dirt.

45

SANU

"Did you think Nasalid would've challenged him to a one-on-one fight?"

"Nasalid is too generous for his own good, but he's not so generous that he'd give his enemy a chance to remove his head."

"He should've killed Steelfur when he had the chance. He had a crossbow in his face and a scimitar on his neck."

"Go chip a tooth. Then the Frengs would have another reason to invade with an even bigger force."

— Overheard chatter as soldiers searched for survivors

Sanu, accompanied by surrendered Sprouter knights and mace-wielding Grovekeeper soldiers, arrived at the Sprouter camp, where Yagub stood sentry.

"Sanu?" Yagub asked. "Is that you?"

Sanu pointed to his damaged ear and then twirled so Yagub could see his injured tail. "Do you know anyone else with an ear like mine or a habit of hurting his tail?"

Yagub let out an awkward half-chuckle, but not like he did around the girl he had a crush on. "What happened?"

"Ridgerd and Nasalid are negotiating a peace treaty," Sanu said. "Or they will, once Ridgerd wakes up. Nasalid put him up in a nice tent and his personal physician is watching over him. We came to tell you and the camp followers that you can join us so you're there when Nasalid and Ridgerd meet."

Several camp followers had arrived to listen, gawking at Nasalid's soldiers in glassy-eyed horror.

Yagub addressed them in Frenglese. "Good King Ridgerd is recovering. It seems that the battle is lost but we are not being taken prisoner."

Sanu came beside him. "Nasalid has enough ships in his fleet to take you all home to Freng or Rotteland."

The camp followers, a mix of blacksmiths, carpenters, tailors, and cooks, murmured among themselves. Sanu turned to the Sprouter knights, who looked much smaller outside their armor. "Can you tell them this isn't a joke? That you know Nasalid is merciful?"

"They already know," one knight said. "The nobles and Saplings paint him as a monster, but that's just so regular rodents will join the cause to invade. Word spread about Nasalid's generosity. I know Qawari, and it sounds like Nasalid's reputation in Freng spread like Ridgerd's reputation in Qawar."

Forgetting himself for a second, Sanu asked, "Do you have a nickname for him like 'Steelfur'?"

The other knights laughed. "We'll think of one. Right now, I'm satisfied with calling him the jird who didn't execute me or my king."

When they finished laughing, the camp followers began packing up their tents and supplies, loading them onto carts. There were barely any foodstuffs that Sanu could see. They wouldn't have lasted much longer. Maybe that was why Ridgerd dropped from exhaustion—knowing him, he probably wasn't eating or drinking as much so others could. Sanu shuddered to consider how many more Grovekeepers Ridgerd would've cut down at full strength.

Yagub in front, the camp followers hauled out, joining Sanu and the soldiers from both sides. The Gnaverwood towered in the distance, an umbrella running up to the sky.

"Should I be glad I missed another battle?" Yagub asked.

"You could've had a mace rupture your guts," Sanu replied, "so I think yes."

"Maybe if I become a Barkheart, I'll experience some real glory on the battlefield."

Sanu sighed. "Against whom? Don't you want this war to end?"

Yagub fell quiet for a moment, eyes on his hindpaws. "Of course I want the war to end.

I guess I had always seen conflict between Sprouters and Grovekeepers as a part of life. But it shouldn't be that way. As a boy, I'd imagined the Barkhearts to be these larger-than-life super warriors for the All-Planter. Maybe I'm better off as a seedling. I wouldn't want to let Brouglas down though." Yagub eyed Sanu and cringed. "Did, um, did Jab tell you about what happened with him?"

Sanu nodded. As much as the news of the beaver knight's death hurt him, he couldn't imagine what kind of pain it must be for Yagub, who'd served as his squire. "I don't think anything you do would let him down if you did your best. He was proud of you."

Sanu wished someone would say that to him about his parents. He hoped they'd be proud of the rodent he was and wanted to become. Even though they were a long way from ZelZaytun, each step brought them closer to his parents' gravesite. Maybe now they could finally rest in peace until Pruning Day.

"Did any of the Barkhearts survive the decoy attack?" Yagub asked.

"Not many," Sanu said. "And I don't know if Nasalid will let them stay in Qawar with their weapons and armor. They're so ruthless. Do you really think the All-Planter approves of them? They destroyed whole towns when they first came. I really don't understand why you'd want to join them."

"I ... hadn't thought of it that way."

"Besides," Sanu said, "if you became a regular seedling, you could go back to Coppergrass.

I remember a certain porcupine you wanted to spend a lot of time with."

A tiny smile crept up Yagub's snout. "You're just full of good ideas, aren't you?"

Sanu shrugged. "What can I say?"

They arrived at the battlefield, where Nasalid's soldiers combed through the fallen, carrying stretchers with Grovekeeper and Sprouter alike. The defeated unarmored Sprouters mostly crouched in shaded spots, sipping on water and watching the Grovekeepers handle the dead. Sanu remembered hearing rodents complain about Nasalid being too generous with the enemy, and he imagined more than a few of the soldiers were thinking the same thing right now.

"Sanu!"

Jab's voice cut through the noise of all the rodents present. Jab hobbled over to them. "King Ridgerd is waking up. Nasalid wants both of us there when they talk. Yagub, you should come too."

Sanu's heart raced, unwilling to admit how scared he'd been that Ridgerd might not wake up.

46

JAB

Seeing the grand architecture and breathtaking art here, I'm ashamed of how many rodents back home referred to the Qawari as savages and the land as a desolate place, saved only by the holy tree. I'll give a stern correction to any Frenglese or Rottelander who speaks poorly about our wonderful neighbors.

- *From the prayer journal of Sir Brouglas*

Jab had heard of insulated jars for holding mountain snow, but he'd never seen one up close. While Ridgerd and Nasalid sitting down in a tent together was a sight to behold, Jab was more than a little distracted by the snow holder. Yagub gaped at it too.

Ridgerd broke eye contact with Nasalid and eyed Jab. "Nasalid offered me snow from the mountains outside Damouscus. It's been quite refreshing. Would you like to sample some, boys?"

Jab looked on hungrily, but he glanced at the Liberator to get a quick nod and smile before approaching the container. Sanu came up beside him. The white stuff practically glowed, and the air itself felt chilled.

"Pinch a bit and put it on your tongue," Nasalid instructed.

Yagub shook his head feverishly.

Undisturbed by the older squirrel, Jab let Sanu take the first pinch, and then followed. The strange stuff was flaky and wet at the same time, dry and cold also. The taste sent a shiver down his tongue, though it had already started melting into water by the time it reached his mouth. Getting this here, still cold, must have been quite a task, no matter how impressive that container. And Nasalid had given this all to Ridgerd, his enemy.

"Did it freeze your tongue?" Yagub whispered.

"You should come to Freng if you're so enamored with snow," Ridgerd said.

Sanu laughed while Jab wondered what "enamored" meant. Jab couldn't imagine himself leaving Qawar again after their misadventure in Coppergrass, though if Rattin were burned down by Rattarossa, he didn't exactly have anywhere to go.

Ridgerd carefully placed the lid back on the snow container, and relaxed back in his seat. The walls of the tent didn't come all the way to the ground, and Jab wondered if Nasalid had ordered this to be built taller to better accommodate Ridgerd's height.

"Are you ready to interpret for us?" Nasalid asked.

Jab tensed. "I'll do my best."

"We all will," Sanu said, pointing to himself and Yagub. "Between the three of us, we won't miss anything."

"Very well," Nasalid said. "Tell him I'm thankful he stopped fighting and has accepted the care of my doctor."

Jab interpreted, and Ridgerd smiled. "And you can tell him that I'm honored to be alive and awake. He could have killed me then or poisoned me here."

Yagub translated, and then added to Ridgerd that the other Frenglese and Rottelander soldiers were being treated kindly as well.

Nasalid thanked Yagub. "Tell the king I understand if he returns with news that he surrendered, he will be ousted, replaced by a worse ruler, and the remaining kings of Freng will demand another invasion. Tell him I do not ask for a surrender but a peace treaty. Thus, he can return saying that he did not get defeated."

After Sanu interpreted, Ridgerd leaned forward. "And what are the proposed terms of this peace treaty?"

Jab took a turn interpreting and eyed the mountain snow, wondering if anyone would notice if he snuck another pinch.

"I'm willing to negotiate of course," Nasalid began, "but I must first know the error my original message contained. I offered peaceful pilgrimage to any Sprouter wishing to visit ZelZaytun. Why was that proclamation met with war?"

Nervous he'd get caught in the middle, Jab interpreted before the others could. He remembered it well. He'd gone with Sanu, Brouglas, and Yagub to deliver the message and they weren't believed. The other nobles and corrupt Sapling convinced Ridgerd it was a trap and pressured him to invade.

Ridgerd let out a long sigh. "That is a fair question. You had two reputations that came to Freng before your message did. One was your generosity, which I can see firstpaw here. The second is your tactical genius. Inviting your strongest enemies to come to Qawar so you could kill them would've been a good plan."

Sanu conveyed that to Nasalid and added that he, Jab, Yagub, and Brouglas had all insisted that it wasn't a trick.

Nasalid rose from his chair and paced the tent, drawing loops in the ground with his tail. "Ask him if he believes me now."

The king tensed, and Yagub tried to soothe him. "Nasalid is frustrated. He'd wanted to avoid an invasion. That's why he's upset. Do you still think he's deceiving you?"

"No," Ridgerd admitted. "He's passed on too many opportunities to kill me for me to think he would now. I will vouch for his honesty back home."

Jab interpreted, and Nasalid finished pacing. "I understand that you've planted olives in Coppergrass, Freng, and Rotteland, and they do not grow as heartily as the Gnaverwood. I'll allow some Qawari soil to go with shipments of olives for use in your Offering Meal rituals. We can meet with the Sapling in ZelZaytun and discuss what holy objects may go with you and Rattarossa's troops to keep in your homelands. Perhaps that will be enough to cool the war dogs." He paused, letting the boys explain. "The rodents of Qawar and the surrounding islands will see me as generous. They will see you as a powerful warrior and a pilgrim."

Ridgerd rose, towering over Nasalid without looming over him. "And we will also make a vow of friendship and aid."

Yagub interpreted, and Jab's hair raised along with his racing heart, sending a fresh wave of pain in his injured hindpaw. He wondered what rubbing some snow on it would do.

"No," Nasalid replied. "I will not tire the Qawari with another war and I won't let either of us get tangled in foreign politics. I have enough dissonance in my ranks. I will call you a friend, but a political alliance feels foolish. We can trade in kindness."

Sanu nudged Jab, whispering "What's 'dissonance' mean?"

By the grace of the All-Planter, Yagub took a turn.

"Ha!" Ridgerd placed a paw on his stomach. "Shrewd! I suppose you're right. If we could combine our strengths in battle, I bet the Great Sea would never know such a force."

Sanu interpreted, and Ridgerd's words made Nasalid smile. "You'll live on in our history as the Steelfur. I hope you live on in your own as the good king. While I once yearned to match wits with you in battle, I hope I can lay down my scimitar forever. Now if we agree to your departure with gifts, might I suggest we first visit the Holy City? You've come all this way. You deserve to see the tree and the Palace of Mulcher Kings."

Jab couldn't believe it. He worried he'd botched his explanation since his smile wouldn't let him say all the words right.

"It is my turn to refuse, Nasalid," Ridgerd replied. "I still have warriors who believe you cannot be trusted and will use this opportunity to kill us."

Jab debated adding that they wouldn't think that if Rattarossa hadn't executed three thousand prisoners, but didn't want to upset the negotiation.

"I can't let a foreign army into the Holy City." Nasalid tsked. After a moment, the jird arched an eyebrow. "What if *you* kept your sword? I doubt any of my soldiers could defeat you in a fight, no matter how outnumbered you were. Your troops' faith in your skill is impressive. Enough so that if *you* entered with sword and shield, they might not see the need for their own, as you have shown yourself to be their ultimate protector."

Jab translated, though he didn't like the idea of Ridgerd keeping his weapon. An image flashed in his mind of the royal hamster stabbing the tree or carving his name into it, but he did his duty.

268 - FAMILIES BROKEN

Ridgerd nodded. "Tell him I will see what my soldiers say, but my hope is that we can see the Holy City together on peaceful terms."

47

SANU

Practicing Grovekeeping in secret is easier than I thought. I have a house in ZelZaytun (I won't write their cursed name for it) that has a basement. My wife and I are free to pray there when we have private time. She's selling sheltercakes from our home and I must say I love how it smells each day. When we're blessed with children, we'll bring them up in this way, preserving our faith and culture in the face of opposition, keeping our tradition alive through food. Maybe our future children will be part of a great overthrow.

- Diaries of General Ironseed's secretary

Sanu didn't watch the city as their giant group approached it. Instead, he watched King Ridgerd and his troops. Wagons hauled away their weapons and armor to be melted down and repurposed or sold, except Ridgerd's of course. Without the armor, the Frenglese and Rottelander soldiers were mere rodents again, no longer the horrifying metal monsters they'd seemed only a few days ago. They were hamsters, porcupines, beavers, dormice, and lemmings—not invaders. They were truly pilgrims now, wearing the Ganan's Rake symbol on clothing instead of armor.

And when they crested the last hill, the city walls came into view.

Ridgerd fell to his knees and wept.

Nasalid strode beside him. "It's a beautiful sight, is it not?" Though mismatched in size, species, and faith, the two generals could've been uncle and nephew for how Nasalid spoke.

Sanu and Jab leaned over in their wagon with a few other injured soldiers. "He asked if you think the city is beautiful," Sanu called.

The royal hamster nodded through whole body sobs. "I-I've wanted this my entire life. So-so long I've had seedlings, Saplings, and my own father swear I would be condemned to the Droughtlands unless I could claim the ultimate victory."

Yagub started to interpret, but Jab put a paw on his arm. "Don't," Jab said. "I think he's saying that to himself. Maybe us. But that's not for Nasalid."

"I think he's right," Sanu said. But Nasalid was staring at him with an eyebrow raised, waiting for the words. "He waited for this moment his whole life."

By now, the whole force had stopped. Wagons, horses, infantry, and camp followers, all in giant columns, stopped and admired ZelZaytun's beauty.

Nasalid looked at Ridgerd again. "Boys, tell him that I once thought myself cursed to the Droughtlands for all the blood on my paws. I believed retaking ZelZaytun would erase my other sins. Tell him that I understand how it feels to worry you are condemned for your actions."

Sanu's mouth dried. He knew that for Ridgerd, his guilt didn't come from something he had done, but from something he was. What that something was, nobody would tell Sanu or Jab, but it did feel different.

Jab had already started. "You and Nasalid are both alike, King Ridgerd. He also believed the city was his one chance at the Walled Garden."

Unashamed of his tears and not bothering to wipe them, the king rose. "Tell Nasalid I can continue to the Holy City now. I won't delay my countryrodents any more than I already have."

Sanu interpreted, and Nasalid called for the mass to continue forward.

When Sanu leaned back in the cart, one of the injured Rottelanders, a stocky lemming, approached them. "You two are close to the king and the jird, yes?"

"Call him the Liberator," Jab corrected. "He's more than his species."

"Sorry," the Rottelander replied. "Habit. What will happen to our weapons and armor? Do you know? I saw you in the tent with them."

"Ridgerd is going to pay you all and donate some money to repair the village Rattarossa burned down," Sanu explained.

"Your armor will be melted down and you can choose not to be paid to keep it instead," Jab said.

The Rottelander ran a paw through his head hair. "What about our swords?"

Sanu strained to remember what Ridgerd and Nasalid had agreed to. "You'll get them back on your boats home."

The large lemming slumped back, and one of his bandages loosened. "Rattarossa didn't have a treasure trove like he promised. I wonder if he ever intended to pay us."

With Barkhearts serving him, Rattarossa probably could've gotten away with not paying them. Sanu wondered what kind of problems or celebrations the Rottelanders would be returning to with only a story about their emperor drowning in a lake to show for it.

Ridgerd and Nasalid, leading the procession, approached the city's main gate.

"Hail, gatekeeper," Nasalid announced. "Note that we are not coming here as victor or vanquished. I have a king on pilgrimage with me, and a large host of fellow pilgrims at our back. They are coming in on my invitation, and they are all unarmed, save my esteemed guest. If any of you in the gatehouse can speak Frenglese, please repeat that for my companion."

When none of the gatekeepers came forward since they were staring in stunned silence, Sanu and Jab hobbled out of the wagon.

The *racka-click* of the rising metal gate gave Sanu chilling memories of crossbows, and he knew it must be worse for Jab.

"King Ridgerd," Sanu said, "He made a point to tell the gatekeeper that neither of you won or lost." He hoped he'd correctly guessed what "vanquished" meant. "He told them that you're all pilgrims and are his guests. They're opening the gate now."

"Thanks, lad." With a weak smile, Ridgerd added, "Though an open gate is the same in any language."

They passed through the city walls, and again, the king sobbed. Their first sight was of a well. Ridgerd knelt before it the same way Grovekeepers knelt in prayer.

"Oh," Jab mused, "there's a story in the *Ganandeeds* that says Ganan had an important conversation with somebody at a well near the city gate. I read it a few days ago. I bet he thinks that's the well."

Sanu arched an eyebrow. "My brother, the guy who wanted to be a prayer warden, is reading the Sprouter holy book?"

Jab nodded. "Remember? Brouglas gave it to me. At first I read it because I felt guilty, but there's good stuff in it. I still want to be a Grovekeeper, but I've liked reading about a different faith. It actually made me understand some things better."

Ridgerd rose from the well, and two other Sprouters took his place. The whole procession diverted so everyone who wanted to could touch or pray at the well.

"We'll be going around the city like this all day, I bet," Sanu said.

"You sound annoyed," Jab replied. "Look at Nasalid. He's smiling. This was what he wanted all along. He wanted Sprouters to come here in peace. I think with Ridgerd experiencing this firstpaw, he can convince everyone back in Freng and Rotteland that Nasalid was serious. This might end religious wars."

Sanu watched Ridgerd, a grown man, strong enough to cut down legions of soldiers in battle, brave enough to stare death in the face, cunning enough to outwit master tacticians, reduced to tears of joy. "Let's get Cladh," Sanu said. "She'll be the last stop on their pilgrimage tonight. I bet she'll prepare something really nice for them in the Gananhall. Then they'll all leave happy."

"Good idea," Jab replied.

The brothers hobbled toward Nasalid, who was still fixated on the Sprouter pilgrims.

"Nasalid," Jab began, "we'd like to visit the Sapling. She should be the last person they see on their trip through the city."

"I agree," Nasalid said. "I don't think I could prevent Sanu from sneaking off to see her anyway."

Sanu's cheeks flushed and he examined his suddenly interesting hindpaws.

Jab chuckled. "Thank you, Liberator. We'll see you tonight? Maybe we could ask the prayer wardens and Mulcher elders to have a big ceremony for the whole city, for all three religions?"

"If they're in agreement, please encourage them," Nasalid said. "Go."

Sanu and Jab headed off toward the city center, passing a group of squirrel kids tossing around a ball. For the first time in months, ZelZaytun wasn't under any threat. Qawar was safe. That hadn't been true since their parents died.

"So, what happens tomorrow?" Sanu asked.

"What do you mean?"

"Rattin is destroyed and the war is over. What's left for us?"

48

JAB

We've heard tell that the Liberator of the other Grovekeeper Isles has set his sights on Qawar. Even the fools in Lady Marjitay's court know it's only a matter of time before he attacks Olihort. Yaqub tells me there's a town where two trade roads intersect called Rattin. I've studied enough military strategy to know he'll take that town. With my lady's and the Sapling's combined permission, I'll ride out there today and beg the townsrodents to shelter in the city. Lord Ganan, Blest be You, please send your favor on this excursion. I won't let what happened at Phranktonbourg happen again.

- from the prayer journal of Sir Brouglas

Jab couldn't stop hearing Sanu's question the rest of the day.

What's left for us?

While they met with Cladh, the question lingered. Making plans for an interfaith ceremony for all the different citizens of ZelZaytun, the question echoed. Even though hearing prayers to the All-Planter in a chorus of different languages overpowered his ears, Sanu's question cut through it all, and Jab felt like he was in a fog. He barely remembered Maimon treating his bandaged hindpaw.

Jab wondered if he was the only rodent in the whole city who didn't sleep easy that night.

Sanu had achieved his dreams of being a great soldier and Jab had been able to learn from great minds of the three faiths, see new islands in the Great Sea, and pray under the liberated Gnaverwood.

All should've been right with the world.

Yet the unknown ate at Jab like a worm tunneling through loose dirt.

Jab made his morning prayers with Sanu and Nasalid. Even though ZelZaytun had prayer halls, most of the Grovekeepers there preferred to pray directly in the Gnaverwood's walled-in grove. Completing his prayers that morning, looking at the fence demarking the olive tree's space, Jab found new meaning in the term "Walled Garden." This beautiful space hadn't been touched by war, though it had come precariously close to it twice in a few months. Both Nasalid and Ridgerd may have ripped the city apart to get at this tree. A pair of jerboas knelt beside one of the roots, beginning their first prayers.

Jab sighed and sat up straight, eyes on Sanu. "Did you figure out what's left for us?" A dry chuckle followed. "Or did you ask because you knew that question would keep me awake all night?"

Sanu scratched the back of his head. "It would've been funny if I'd come up with something just to keep you from sleeping, but ... I asked because I thought you'd know. You're the smart one."

Jab smiled. "I wish I was smart enough to know."

Nasalid completed his prayer and rose. "Boys, you have your whole lives in front of you. The Great Sea is in your paws."

Didn't he know that was the scary part?

"We're orphans, Nasalid," Jab said. "Our hometown was burned."

"Since our parents died, we've just been going along with what's happening around us." Sanu rose on shaky legs and then offered a paw to help Jab stand. "At the Battle of Rattin, Brouglas took me, you took Jab, then bad winds took us to Coppergrass, and Ridgerd brought us back here."

"And now it's up to you," Nasalid replied, gesturing toward the tree. "Would you like to live here? Help rebuild Rattin? I could adopt you both and bring you back to Damouscus with me and Dilaal." His gaze lowered. "And I suppose if you tire of Qawar, Ridgerd would take you to Freng with him, though I can't promise you peace there."

Jab chewed on his lower lip. Those all sounded like good options, though he wasn't sure he wanted to meet Ridgerd's little brother. A little bit away from them, a small family of gerbils prayed by the tree. He wondered what kind of relationship those siblings had with each other.

"That's what we're saying," Sanu protested. "We don't know what to do. We've never had this many options."

Wafts of cinnamon danced in the air. Somebody was making sheltercake nearby.

Nasalid headed toward the city center and the main Gananhall. "Let's at least see off the Frenglese and Rottelanders. King Ridgerd did request to bid you both farewell, though I suspect he also wishes to invite you back to Freng with him. Their Offering Meal should be concluded soon."

They kept quiet on the short walk there, and Jab fixated on Sanu saying that Brouglas had "taken" him. Brouglas saved Sanu's life that night. He then saved Jab's life by diving into the Great Sea and swimming after him. He saved Jab's life again by fighting off Rattarossa. Reading the beaver knight's prayer journal along with his holy book revealed many things in his noble heart. As they approached the Gananhall, Jab eyed his brother.

What if he and Sanu wanted different things? What if they didn't want to do the same thing?

They'd been apart and had adventures, but those had only been for a month at a time. Even though it hurt, Jab realized he and his brother could want and pursue different things in life. Twins or not, they were still their own squirrels.

The Gananhall's bell rang, a brassy echo noting the end of a ritual.

"Sanu," Jab began, "I have something I need to tell you before we meet Ridgerd and Cladh again."

Nasalid bowed his head and strode forward, allowing them some space.

Jab held Sanu's wrist and they both stopped. A sunbird fluttered down near them, settling on a flower, tweeting happily.

"Did you figure something out?" Sanu asked.

"I want to honor Sir Brouglas."

"How?"

Jab reached into his tunic and pulled out the beaver knight's prayer journal, the leather binding smooth in his paws. "He had a brother. Something happened between them. He told me about it and he wrote it down. They'd grown apart over the years. He kept writing to him, but he never got any responses."

Sanu's whiskers drooped. "That's so sad." He breathed deep and stiffened, putting a fist over his heart. "No matter how mad at you I get, I'll always answer your letters. Even if you're being a pellet eater."

"You'll answer my letters?" Jab asked. "Does that mean you wouldn't be mad at me if we went to different places? Because I think I know what I want to do, but I don't want to make you come with me if it's not what you want."

Sanu folded his arms. "I hadn't thought about it, but you're right. I think we can still be good brothers even if we're not next to each other. I know I didn't really appreciate you until I thought you were dead."

Jab chuckled, knowing that King Ridgerd would bark out a "Ha!" if he'd been there. "I want to find Sir Brouglas's brother. I think Brouglas's family should know what kind of a knight he was. I think his is a story that should be remembered. I don't know if that means going to Freng or Rotteland or back to Coppergrass, but I'm not afraid of searching. Even if it takes years."

Sanu stared at his hindpaws, and a light breeze rustled to fill the silence between them, despite the chatter of the horde of Sprouters leaving the Gananhall.

"Jab?"

"Yeah?"

"I don't know if Nasalid and his brother or Ridgerd and his can truly fix what's broken their families. I'd like to think Nasalid will forgive Dilaal, but I bet he's taking him to Damouscus so he can keep an eye on him. Ridgerd might be going home to a civil war against his brother. Brouglas and his brother though? That's the only relationship that can't get worse. I want to come with you. There's too much hurt for me in Qawar."

Jab's heart stuck in his throat. Sanu was definitely the smart one. Jab had no desire to stay in Qawar, since this was the place of his greatest nightmares and heartache. "That's what we'll do then," Jab said.

With confidence that mighty King Ridgerd would do the same, Jab didn't resist the tears coming. "Let's find his family. And restore it."

The Great Sea is a big place with lots of islands brimming with different cultures and conflicts. Check out more adventures in the Gnaverworld! Look for the *Ghosts and Iron* trilogy.

BOOK CLUB QUESTIONS

1. How did Sanu and Jab's images of Ridgerd and Nasalid change?

2. Was Nasalid right to use up all of Qawar's resources to keep his soldiers safe? Explain.

3. Did your opinion of either brother change from the earlier books? Why?

4. Of all the "broken families" do you think the Sprouters and Grovekeepers count as one? Explain whether you think they'll be able to get along now.

5. Between Ridgerd and his brother, and Nasalid and his, do you expect any of them to fix their relationships?

6. Sanu and Jab met some helpful friends and dangerous foes in their journeys. Which side character was your favorite and why?

7. If you were in Sanu and Jab's position at the end of the book, what would you have done?

8. Is Yagub a traitor to Qawar or a loyal Sprouter? Explain.

9. What was your favorite part of the book?

10. Do you think Sanu and Jab will find Brouglas's brother? How do you think that meeting will go?

AUTHOR BIO

PC is a fantasy and science fiction author from the Great Lakes region of the USA. Fantasy has been a deep love for PC, growing up on Star Wars movies and reading the Redwall series. The Star Wars novels along with fantasy greats like Brandon Sanderson, C.S. Lewis, and Tolkien are constant sources of inspiration and wonder. PC loves taking his daughters to the zoo and the occasional sushi or taco date with his wife. With the help of historians and martial artists, PC tries to blend real historical elements with some great rodent action in his stories. Tune in to the Radio Freewrite podcast every Friday to hear original works by PC. Visit PC's website at authorpcnottingham.com and sign up for the newsletter for updates and exclusive content!

**Discover more at
4HorsemenPublications.com**

10% off using HORSEMEN10

www.ingramcontent.com/pod-product-compliance
Lightning Source LLC
LaVergne TN
LVHW041751060526
838201LV00046B/971